THE WHISTLING SANDS

A NED FLYNN CRIME THRILLER

MATH BIRD

MCSNOWELL BOOKS

Copyright © 2015-2021 by Math Bird

All rights reserved.

This book is a work of fiction. Names, characters, places, and incidents are the product of the author's imagination or are used fictitiously, and any resemblance to actual events, places or persons, living or dead, is entirely coincidental.

No part of this book may be reproduced in any form or by any electronic or mechanical means, including information storage and retrieval systems, without written permission from the author, except for the use of brief quotations in a book review.

For Yan.

PART I

SOMEBODY TO LOVE

1

If death wore a mask, then Ned Flynn's mother had stolen it. She was pale, emaciated, and her brown eyes, which had once shone with exuberance, looked haunted. She hadn't seemed that bad when she'd visited him in prison. That was months ago, and yesterday was the first time he'd seen her since his release. He would have come home sooner if he'd known, broken his probation. She looked so happy as she greeted him at the door. All he did was stare, and this morning, as they sat at the kitchen table, he kept asking if she was all right.

'I'm fine,' she insisted, but they both knew it to be untrue.

'You need to rest,' Flynn said.

His mother raised her eyes. 'Rest doesn't pay the bills or buy food.' She stared into her cup and sighed. 'I'll have plenty of time to rest when I'm in the ground, until then I need to keep working.'

Flynn reached across the table and touched his mother's hand. 'I'm going to help you with that.'

His mother smiled. 'So you said. Have you won the lottery?'

Flynn laughed. 'I wish.' He studied the hopelessness in her eyes. 'I'm going to see a man about a job. It's good money too.'

His mother shot him a wary glance. 'And who might that be?'

'John Mason.'

She closed her eyes and sighed. 'Did you learn nothing in prison, Ned? You've barely been back a day and you're already selling yourself cheap to that jumped-up wannabe.'

Flynn squeezed his mother's hand. 'It's not like that. I want to help you. I know it's not ideal, but we all need to make sacrifices.'

'If you say so. A nice girl you want. A good woman can be the making of a man.'

Flynn glanced down at the table. 'I tried that and look where it got me, spent two years in Walton because of it.'

'I don't mean *her*. A *nice* girl, I said. Your trouble is that you always chase after the wrong type. Looks aren't everything.' She pulled her hand free and rested it on her face. 'Mason's wife ran off, you know. He's bad news, Ned. I'd steer clear if I were you. He's a nasty piece of work. No good will come of it.'

2

When Flynn arrived at the big white house, Mason stood waiting by the gate. 'Thanks for coming, Flynn,' he said, then lit a cigarette.

They made an odd pairing. Mason looked frail, an old man with blonde highlights, dressed too young for his age. Not that Flynn looked any better, towering over him, a lumbering giant dressed in his father's old suit.

Mason took a drag of his cigarette. 'I suppose you've heard about my wife and me?'

Flynn nodded. 'It's hard not to, especially in a town as small as this.'

Mason reached into his pocket, his hand trembling slightly as he pulled out a sheet of paper. 'After she ran off, I heard nothing for months. Then this arrived two days ago.' He waved the letter in front of him, then held it to his chest as though guarding some dark secret. 'Nia's in a place called Aberdaron. It's up west, along the coast.'

Mason's voice crackled when he mentioned his wife's name. 'She says she owes money everywhere, got herself into a right mess.'

Flynn straightened. 'Do you want me to take her some?'

Mason stubbed out his cigarette. 'Hell, no, it's time that girl came home. I want you to fetch her back.' He studied Flynn for a moment. 'Keep it to yourself. I don't want people thinking I'm a fool. This job stays between you and me.'

'What do you want me to say to her?'

Mason shrugged. 'I don't know. A man with your talents should find it easy enough to persuade her.' He tapped his pocket. 'There's three grand here that tells me you'll think of something.'

'Three grand?'

Mason grinned. 'You'll get the rest on delivery, think of it as a down payment.' He scrunched the letter in his hand, flipped open his lighter, then set it alight. He watched it burn for a while, dropping it to the ground as the flames snapped at his fingers. 'You keep that temper under control, Flynn. Don't be rough with her.'

Flynn frowned. 'I've never hurt a woman in my life. It's been the other way around, if anything.'

Mason gave him a flat smile. 'Glad to hear it.' He reached into his inside pocket and took out a thick, brown envelope. 'This guy she's with, Haines, you can be as rough with him as you like. I never want him to come near her again.'

Flynn nodded, staying silent as he scanned the big white house. The place was too big for one man. There were too many rooms, too many echoes, and if the rumours about Mason were true, too many dark shadows. He thought about his time inside and all the promises he'd made himself. He'd vowed never to do another man's bidding, find some honest work, and keep himself clear of the drink. The planning of his life had always proved so much easier than its living. Men like Mason knew that; and as Flynn snatched the envelope from his hand, he glimpsed something in the old man's eyes that told him Mason could read him like a book.

As the minutes passed, Flynn's dislike for Mason grew stronger. The old man was too sure of himself. Money had given him too many privileges. Flynn had met his type so many times before. Guys who had done a few dodgy deals, convincing themselves they were big-shot gangsters. Flynn knew the real thing, and John Mason didn't come close. To make things worse, the old man insisted Flynn took the train.

'Can't you just lend me a car?' Flynn asked.

'Sure, if you hand over your licence.'

'You know I don't have one.'

'Exactly,' Mason said with a grin. 'You're fresh out of prison. What if you get stopped? I want this done right. Let's not take any chances.'

3

Flynn caught the village of Aberdaron out of season. The holiday homes stood vacant in the aftermath of the morning rain, as despondent seabirds watched him from the glistening rooftops. They made a mournful sound, those church bells by the sea, holding him silent as he gazed across the water. As Flynn strolled through the village, all he could think about was Haines. He'd never met the man, but he'd heard so much about him. Haines was a minister, a charmer, or so he'd been told, a spinner of yarns, especially when the drink got the better of him. Flynn knew the type. Their faces always shaved and scented, every other word leading them into prayer. Haines had probably convinced Nia into joining the Methodist church, luring her into bed with his hymns and his verses. Flynn knew the type all right and pictured a man pleased with himself, basking in his spoils, and unaware of danger.

The White Lion Hotel was pleasant enough. Whitewashed and low-roofed, its dark oak furnishings complimented the floral carpet. After checking into his room,

Flynn ventured into the bar. One drink couldn't do any harm, or so he convinced himself.

The barman greeted him with a smile, eyeing him slyly as he poured his pint. 'You've picked the wrong time of year to come, holiday season's over.'

Flynn nodded. 'Who says I'm on holiday.'

The barman smiled. 'Are you visiting friends?'

Flynn sighed. 'If you must know I'm on business.'

'That's £3.50,' the barman said. 'Listen, I didn't mean to pry. I was just trying to be friendly.'

Flynn handed him a five pound note. 'No worries, I'm the same, Welsh curiosity.'

The barman handed him his change. '*Welsh*, I thought you were from Liverpool?'

Flynn got this wherever he went. People questioning where he was from just because he didn't have a Welsh accent. The Welsh were the worst, especially as you went further west.

'I'm from the Northeast,' Flynn said, 'you know, the border.'

The barman grinned. 'Yeah, I know it, like I said, Liverpool.'

Flynn considered leaning over the bar and giving him a slap. He could have easily grabbed the barman's hair and smashed his face down on the counter. The barman would be unconscious before he hit the floor, blood and snot on his face, a big wet patch around his crotch. Instead, Flynn picked up his pint, smiled, and walked away, leaving such thoughts to the confines of his imagination.

Except for the barman, the people in the pub took no notice of him, throwing him the odd smile whenever he caught their glance. Experience had taught him he shouldn't waste his time. He needed to take Nia back; convince her it was for the best. But one pint couldn't do any harm, especially when the weather was so bleak. It would calm him down, stop him fretting about his mother and keep those black moods at bay.

4

Flynn woke at daybreak. It was invariably the case when he'd been drinking. Everyone was still asleep, and an eerie silence had descended over the place. After grabbing a quick shower, he went for a walk, heading to the beach to kill a few hours before breakfast. He mooched along the shore, watching the pebbles glistening beneath the dawn light. The sky was so clear, an infinite sweep of blue that he hadn't seen for some time. He felt tiny against the vastness of the sea. He was nothing compared to these rocks, mere flesh, and bone, defenceless against the ferocity of the tide.

Flynn picked up a pebble and skimmed it across the water, glancing at a dog's paw marks chasing off into a patch of wet sand. It reminded him of his father, and that one holiday they had when he was a kid. They went to a place down the coast, a shabby seaside resort, like this one. It started as fun until the weather changed, and his father began drinking. He remembered his father trying to teach him how to swim, finally losing patience, pushing his head under the water. The memory lived with him for years. He hadn't been to a beach since. Well, not until today. But even this place was starting to get under his skin.

5

When he arrived back at the hotel, except for an old couple, the dining room was empty. The weather had turned so quickly, and a leaden sky loomed behind the windows, greying the walls and curtains. At least the waitress was cheery, her eyes illuminated by that unblemished shine of youth. She set a pot of coffee on the table. 'Are you here for your holidays?'

Flynn shook his head, 'Visiting a friend.' She looked at him for a moment, waiting for him to continue. Her cheeks burned as he watched her in silence. She twiddled a button on her blouse. 'Well, I hope you have a lovely time,' she said and turned towards another table.

Flynn tapped her arm, offering her his best smile as she spun around. He reached into his pocket, drew out a slip of paper and pointed at Nia's address. 'I don't suppose you can help me?'

Her face looked older as she gazed down at it, her breath warm as she murmured through the address. 'If it's the Garreg Cottage, I'm thinking of, it's just past Mansion woods.'

'Is it far?'

'Depends, it's awkward to get there by car. If it were me, I'd take the shortcut along the coastal path. It's a beautiful walk, even on a day like this.'

'And I just follow it?'

'Yeah, until you get to the crossroads. Then take a right onto the road. The cottage is on your left.'

'Sounds easy.'

She smiled. 'I hope so, but if you come to a bay called Hell's Mouth, you've taken the wrong path.'

'I'll bear that in mind,' Flynn said, almost telling her he'd been taking the wrong path all his life.

6

Flynn kept to the route, just as the waitress had told him; mindful of every turn in case he strayed from the path. The journey took longer than he expected, and it was late afternoon before he reached the crossroads. At least he'd found it and feeling pleased with himself he confidently took a right. The road, as the waitress described it, was little more than a stretch of tarmac. Lines of trees towered on either side, their hanging branches almost black against the waning light.

There was no trace of the cottage and feeling tired of the never-ending road, Flynn decided to head back. As he turned around, he took sight of a narrow lane veering off into the trees. He must have missed it when he first walked past. He inched closer and on seeing a distant light glimmer through the darkness, the drudgery lifted from his shoulders and his heart felt a tinge of hope.

The light drew him deeper into the woods, and he chased after it, breaking into a jog.

Flynn stopped to catch his breath; each deep swallow of air burned inside his chest. Except for the dim sketch of light, the woods lay immersed in blackness. The wind rose; its sudden gust swept unexpectedly through the naked branches. A dank chill hung in the air. Flynn turned up his collar, turning his head swiftly to the sound of something snapping in the grass.

On catching sight of the pale, grim face, Flynn's heart throbbed inside his throat. His mouth turned dry and when asking, 'Hey, fella, what the hell are you thinking, creeping up on people like that?' he struggled to get his words out.

The stranger didn't respond. He stood and stared, his sleek hair black like the night, his chiseled jawline smeared with five o'clock shadow.

Flynn clenched his fists. 'I asked you a question; what's wrong, the cat got your tongue?'

The man stood silently, treading back into the trees the moment Flynn stepped towards him.

Out in the open, Flynn would have darted towards him. Yet here, among the confines of the trees, all he could do was plough his way helplessly through the branches, allowing the stranger to gain more distance.

Flynn chased after him, a vain gesture, stopping when the stranger vanished into the gloom. 'I'll see you again,' he called out, disturbed by the fearful hint in his own voice.

Flynn raked his fingers through his hair. 'Jesus,' he said through a sigh, his hand trembling slightly as he lit a cigarette. He smoked it down to a stub, flicked it into the grass and retraced his steps, that ghostly glimmer of light guiding him through the darkness.

7

Garreg Cottage stood hidden against a backdrop of trees; its windows glowed in the darkness, and tufts of smoke wafted from the chimney. Flynn hammered at the door, gazing up when someone opened the top window. Even dragged from sleep, Nia looked stunning. She had strong cheekbones and green eyes, her long silky brown hair resting gently against the pale hues of her skin.

Flynn just stood and stared; it didn't seem to trouble her, and he could tell by the look in her eyes she was used to it.

'Who are you?' she said.

'Ned Flynn.'

She tilted her head to one side as though trying to place him. 'What do you want?'

'Your husband sent me. Wanted me to speak with you about a recent letter you wrote.'

It seemed enough to convince her, and as she disappeared from the window, Flynn patted down his clothes and stamped the mud from his boots. Moments later, she opened the door and let him inside. It felt great to be indoors. The cottage was warm and the air smoky.

She looked at him and smiled. 'I remember you now. Mad Flynn. Isn't that what they used to call you?'

Flynn hated the name and all the baggage that followed it. He sought to make light of it. 'Some still do, those stupid enough to believe the stories.'

'And which stories are those, the one where you bit a man's ear off?'

He laughed. 'It's all fuzzy, to be honest with you. Most of that took place when I was drinking.'

'You don't drink anymore?'

'No,' he lied. 'No ... not as much.'

She didn't answer, and he followed her gaze as she looked down at the carpet, her eyes resting on his muddy footprints.

'I'm sorry,' he said, 'got lost in the woods, had quite a night of it.'

She gestured towards the lounge. 'Wait in here; I'll get you a drink; you look shattered.'

Flynn took off his boots and followed her into the lounge.

'Sit down', she said and went to the kitchen.

Flynn slumped onto the sofa, trying not to close his eyes as the heat from the fire washed over him.

8

The last thing Flynn remembered was sipping from a hot mug of tea. It must have been a deep sleep, because when he woke it was already morning.

'Did I disturb you?' Nia said.

He shook his head, eyeing her shape as she drew back the curtains. He could see why Mason was so desperate to get her back. She was something, those long legs, her hair, face, shoulders, breasts and hips, every curve perfectly in place. He could have watched her forever; it seemed a sin and a shame to take her back.

Flynn yawned and wiped the sleep from his eyes, casting such thoughts aside, trying to focus his mind on business. He looked at her and smiled. 'I guess you know why I'm here?'

Nia sighed and sat in the chair opposite. 'Yes, but you'd think if he loved me that much, he'd come himself.'

'Maybe he didn't feel up to it. He didn't look too good the last time I saw him.'

She raised her eyes. 'Don't let him fool you. The only thing wrong with him is that he can't take no for an answer.'

'All I know is that he wants you home, sent me to fetch you.'

'And if I won't come?'

Flynn glanced down at his hands. 'I'll have to persuade you.' He watched the certainty fade from Nia's eyes, and knowing she'd understood, asked, 'So where is he then?'

'Who?'

'Preacher-boy, this new man of yours.'

The colour drained from Nia's face. 'Martin's... Martin's dead; it's been a month now.'

Flynn sat up. It seemed odd to hear Haines referred to by his first name, almost as though he was another person. 'I'm sorry to hear that.' He wasn't, but he said it all the same.

'Don't be. We're still together. I still talk to him through prayer.'

Flynn hesitated, not knowing how to answer. 'What happened?'

Nia twisted a strand of hair around her finger. 'He drowned on one of his late-night swims.'

'Were you with him?'

She shook her head. 'No, a local boy saw him. All they found were his clothes scattered across the sands.'

A tear crept down her cheek, and before Flynn could check himself, he leaned forward and touched her hand, caressing it with his thumb. He followed the rise and fall of her chest, squeezing her hand tighter, then releasing it to the sudden slam of the garden gate.

As Flynn stood up, Nia grabbed his arm. 'It's only Bevan; he's harmless. He's been helping me out.'

'What with?'

'Stuff. He's a local handyman, gamekeeper, spends most of his time in the woods.'

A shiver ran down Flynn's spine as he pictured the

stranger watching him in the trees. 'I think we've already met,' he said and followed Nia to the door.

The face that greeted him was not the one he expected. Bevan was much older. His cheeks were pink, and small red veins covered his nose, and a grey fringe straggled from the lip of his blue cap. He fixed Flynn with a glare. 'Who are you?' Before Flynn could answer, Nia stepped between them. 'This is Ned Flynn, Bevan. He's an acquaintance of my ex-husband.'

Bevan mumbled something beneath his breath, then took out a rizla, loaded it with tobacco, and rolled it into a cigarette.

'Here,' Flynn said, flicking open his lighter.

Bevan put the cigarette behind his ear. 'No thanks. I'll smoke it later.' He flashed Nia a smile. 'I'll be off then. I just called to see if you needed anything from the village?'

Nia shook her head. 'No, I'm fine, but Ned's staying at the White Lion. Perhaps you can give him a lift back?'

'No, Nia,' Flynn said. 'We need to–'

'Can we discuss it later, Ned? Why don't you check out of your hotel and come and stay here for a few days as my guest?'

9

The Land Rover reeked of petrol, and each time Bevan sighed, he added to Flynn's discomfort with the sourness of his breath. Preferring the cold to the smell, Flynn wound down the window.

Bevan drove like a snail, drawing on his cigarette, his shark eyes skimming between Flynn and the road. He took one last deep drag and flicked his cigarette out of the window. 'Where do I know you from, Flynn? I've seen your face somewhere.'

Flynn shrugged and patted the ash from his clothes. 'I don't know. Perhaps you've seen me somewhere else. How long have you lived here?'

'Too long,' Bevan said, and both men exchanged a smile.

Potholes riddled the winding narrow road, and every sudden jolt churned up Flynn's guts.

Bevan cast him a glance. 'What brings you up here?'

'Business.' Bevan smiled. 'Is that right, and what business might that be?'

'My own business.' A bird darted across the window, causing Bevan to press hard on the brakes. Flynn lunged forward, doubting if the old man had done it on purpose. Bevan took a deep breath, gripped the steering wheel, and carried on driving. 'Sorry about that,' he said with a grin. 'I hope you didn't shit your pants.'

Flynn shook his head and smiled. 'I thought that was you. In fact, by the smell of your breath, I thought you might have had it for breakfast.'

Bevan sighed. 'You're quick with your answers.'

'Yeah, I'm quick with my hands too.'

'What's that supposed to mean?'

'Take it how you like, think of it as a friendly warning.'

'A warning against what?'

'Poking your nose into people's business.'

Bevan eased off the gas. 'I'm just looking out for Nia. I'm extremely fond of her.'

'I bet you are.'

Bevan threw Flynn a furious look. 'Not in that sense. She's like a daughter to me. God help anyone who tries to harm her.'

'What makes you think anyone will?'

'Stuff.'

'What stuff?'

Bevan stopped at a junction, then took a right onto the village road. 'You showing up for one; all that stuff she went through with Haines and all the trouble she had in the village.'

'What trouble?'

Bevan took one hand off the wheel and reached into his pocket for a cigarette. He popped it into his mouth. 'It's not for me to say,' he said, then drove the rest of the way in silence.

10

When Flynn and Bevan returned to the cottage, Nia was out. Bevan unlocked the door, and Flynn followed him inside. They waited in the lounge, the midday sun filling the room with light. One of Nia's top rested on the back of a chair, its scent lingering as though she was still in the room. Bevan glanced at it, then shuffled in his seat. 'She won't be long; she's out walking.'

Flynn nodded. 'Where does she go?'

'The coastal path, then down to the Whistling Sands.'

'*Whistling Sands?*' Flynn scoffed.

Bevan laughed. 'Yeah, it's the sound it makes when you walk there, the shape of the grains or something. Porthor Beach is its proper name. It's a remote spot, especially around this time. Nia goes there every day.' He hesitated for a moment. 'She and Haines used to love the place.'

'Is that where he–'

Bevan nodded. 'Yeah, it's a sad state of affairs. He was no saint mind.'

'How did you come to know him?'

'Through work, I did some jobs for him when he first

moved here. You know what Haines was like. He could talk you into anything. Not that he paid me that much. Mostly I did it as a favour, for Nia's sake. I guess I felt sorry for her.'

'Why?'

'Well, he had that look about him, didn't he?'

'What look?'

'The look women like, tall, dark, square-jawed, you know what I mean, you've seen him.'

Flynn remained silent, picturing the stranger's face in the woods.

11

Nia arrived home just after one-thirty. Bevan made an excuse about some unfinished work, said his goodbyes, and left them alone. Flynn felt awkward at first. He didn't know where to put himself. In the space of a day, he'd gone from intruder to guest. If it wasn't for the money, he would have left her alone. Collecting unpaid debts was more his kind of thing. Yet here he was receiving the grand tour of the house.

Flynn followed Nia upstairs; his eyes fixed on the sway of her hips. He wanted to reach out and take hold of her, but the voice in his head told him not to touch. She showed him to his room. The bed was enormous, with four plump pillows and fresh linen sheets. 'Just treat the place like your home,' she said. 'I know you're here to fetch me back. But I can see a tenderness in your eyes. At least listen to my side of it. I hope we can be civil about all this.'

Flynn nodded, glancing into the mirror as he dropped his bag onto the carpet. He still had a handsome face, a little worse for wear perhaps. He kept his hair short, tried to hide his scars beneath his five o'clock shadow. Women either loved or hated his face; there was no in-between. He wondered what Nia thought, if anything else lay behind the kindness of her smile?

'This is great,' he said, growing more uneasy as she watched him in silence.

'Good. I'm glad you like it.' She shot him that bewitching smile. 'The bathroom's across the landing. Why don't you freshen up while I make us something to eat?'

F lynn was quiet during dinner. All he wanted to do was finish the job and get home. But Nia wanted to have her say. He figured he owed her that much. Besides, he was content to let her jabber on. He'd never been one for conversation.

'So, tell me,' Nia said, 'how much is my husband paying you?' Flynn pushed the meat around his plate. 'Enough,' he said, glancing up.

Her eyes met his. 'What did he say about me?'

Flynn shrugged. 'Nothing much. He mentioned you needed money. That you've got yourself into a mess.'

She banged down her fork, scraped back her chair, and strode over to the window. She gazed outside. 'You know, I begged him to come here himself, to talk things through. It's the least he owes me.' She turned around to face him. 'I'm not in a *mess*, Ned. I've a few debts. Who hasn't for God's sake?'

Flynn held up his palms. 'Hey, don't shoot the messenger. I'm just telling you what he told me.'

She closed her eyes for an instant. 'I'm sorry, but he always tries to twist things.'

Flynn nodded. 'Hmm, he seemed desperate to me.'

'So was I, to get away from him. He just hates to lose, treats people like his property.'

'So why were you so keen to see him then?'

She walked over to the table and grabbed the back of a chair, pressing her weight into it, her blouse stretching across her chest. 'Some stupid notion, I guess. I haven't been myself, not since Martin . . . I just thought I could explain things to him.' Her green eyes flashed with anger. 'He owes me, Ned. You don't know the half of it.'

12

In the evening, they listened to music. Flynn chose the tracks. He kept playing Jefferson Airplane's *Somebody to Love*. The song reminded him of when he was a kid, one of mother's favourites. Nia sat close to him, and he could feel the rise and fall of her chest. Each slight touch excited him, but he tried hard not to stare at her, his eyes fixed on the fire, picturing her body from memory.

Outside, the wind wailed through the trees, and a shadow of leaves quivered across the window. Flynn studied the oil painting above the fireplace: an old woman dying in her bed, a younger version of herself watching over her.

'It was a gift from the artist,' Nia said. 'She used to come to the church. It's valuable, I think.'

'What's it supposed to mean?'

'It shows how life's continuous.'

Flynn nodded, uncertain how to respond.

She shifted closer and grabbed his hand. 'It's all right. I know what you're thinking.'

He grinned. 'And what's that?'

'That I'm crazy. I used to think the same until Martin renewed my faith.'

He didn't like her speaking about Haines, but didn't comment on it, and tried his best to appear unruffled. 'You must miss him a lot.'

She glanced at the window. 'I do, but I still talk to him.'

'I'm sorry?'

'Here, and out on the sands, he speaks to me, comes to me through prayer.'

13

Later that night Nia came to him, floating into his room like a ghost. She lay naked on his bed and pushed against him. He'd been awake thinking of her and was ready when her hand strayed beneath the sheet. She leaned over and kissed his neck, then his chest, his stomach, slowly working her way down.

Her mouth was soft and warm, as was each flick of her tongue. He swallowed each gasp for breath. Years of confinement had taught him to keep his pleasures silent. She lifted her head, pressed her hands into the mattress and eased herself onto him. Flynn closed his eyes for a moment as he felt himself inside her. Her breasts were large and firm, and after rubbing her hands up and down her thighs, she smoothed her cheek across her shoulder, her skin glowing as it took the light.

14

The next morning, Flynn woke up alone. Light poured through the window, exposing the creases on Nia's pillow. The smell of her perfume lingered; the thought of her stirred something inside him, a restless feeling, dragging him out of bed. He dressed hastily and made his way onto the landing. Shivering against the crisp air, he glimpsed at the curtain flapping against the bathroom window.

He raced downstairs and strayed from room to room, calling out Nia's name, only to find the house deserted. Flynn wandered into the kitchen. Water dripped from the tap, and a half-drunk cup of tea stood abandoned on the table. He drew back a chair and sat down; Nia's absence filled him with an insatiable sense of loss. To kill time, he took out his phone and thumbed through a list of missed calls. They were all from Mason, as were the countless texts and voice messages. Flynn listened to them all, shaking his head, as Mason's voice grew more agitated. The old man's voice trembled with every threat. '*You better call me, Flynn. What the hell are you up to?*'

After deleting all the messages, Flynn considered whether to call Mason back. What would he tell him? Haines was dead. That Nia had bedded a better man, and no longer wanted him. Flynn pictured her lying next to him, hoping it wasn't a dream. When he heard the front door open, he rushed into the hall. He greeted her with a smile, but much to his disappointment, Nia didn't smile back. Instead, she looked straight through him as though she were looking at someone else.

'Are you all right?' he said, but she refused to answer.

He followed her into the lounge, sat beside her, saying nothing as she stared into the fire. It was the second time he'd seen her like this. It was as though she'd lost a part of herself. And no matter how hard he tried, she seemed inconsolable. He knelt in front of her and held her hands. Her fingers were icy, her face pale against the morning's grey light. Flynn looked into her eyes, searching for a trace of the woman who had come to him last night. What did she see out on those sands? Whose memory held her silent?

'Nia,' Flynn kept saying, until she eventually acknowledged him; her eyes grew brighter, and Flynn couldn't contain his smile as he stared at that wonderful face. He realised why Mason was so desperate to get her back. Flynn shared the old man's anguish and that look of yearning in Mason's eyes was now his.

15

Each night, Flynn lay with her in his bed. After they'd made love, he listened to the softness of her breath, or whisper her name. Sometimes he'd wake up alone and watch her shadow across the landing. He listened to the murmur of her prayers, heard her asking God for strength. She sang the saddest songs, hymns mostly. The sweetness of her voice was haunting. Yet he knew her words were for Haines; the thought nettled him, and he wished each prayer would be her last.

16

Flynn put his arm around her shoulder. 'Come on, Nia, you've been acting like this for days now, just tell me what's wrong.'

She wiped the tears from her eyes. 'I've got things on my mind.'

'What things?'

She squeezed his hand. 'Just stuff, Mason, you and me, how I'm going to pay the rent.'

'How much do you owe?'

'Two months, the landlord's given me till Thursday.'

'What landlord?'

'Mr Simmons, he owns the estate agents in the village.'

'Can't he give you more time?'

She shrugged. 'He was understanding, at first, until–'

'Until what?'

'Until I fell out with some people in the village and they started talking.'

Flynn laughed. 'You must have *some* friends there? You can't have fallen out with everyone.'

She stared at him. 'They're a strange sort around here. They're all so...'

'What?'

'Changeable.'

Flynn stood and went upstairs. When he came back into the room, he was holding a small paper bag. He rested on his haunches, ripped open the bag and let a bundle of notes spill onto the table. 'Take two grand from that. It should cover four months' rent at least.'

Nia's eyes widened. 'Where did you get it from?'

'Mason gave it to me as an advance.'

'Two thousand pounds, is that all I'm worth to him?'

'Actually, he gave me three. But that's just a percentage. I get the rest on delivery.'

She closed her eyes an instant. 'I can't take this money, Ned.'

He leaned forward and grabbed her arms, 'Why not? You said he owes you. Think of it as repayment.'

'I can't do that; it's all you've got.'

'It still leaves me with a grand. This money's ours now. Please, let me help you.'

She stroked his cheek. 'You've got a good heart, Ned, no matter what anyone says.'

17

The rain fell like a scourge, drenching the fields and sullying the distant sands. Nothing stirred in the trees, and the seabirds cowered among the high rocks. Nia refused to accompany Flynn to the village, so he went alone. The place looked bleak. Water spewed from the drains, and the air stank as he traipsed through the polished streets. Simmons Estate Agents was just beyond the bridge, a low-lit converted cottage, on the edge of a narrow street. Before going in, Flynn peered through the window, happy to find Simmons alone. He swung open the door and strode inside, the doorbell jangling behind him.

Simmons, his face creased and tanned, watched from behind his desk. He removed his glasses, rubbed his eyes, then smoothed his hand across the thin white curls brushed across his balding head. 'Please,' he said and gestured towards the chair opposite.

Flynn sat down, dripping water onto the carpet.

'Wretched weather,' Simmons said. 'How can I help you?'

Flynn pulled a package out of his pocket and slapped it on the desk.

Simmons scanned the torn paper bag with a disapproving eye. He put on his glasses. 'What's this?' Flynn forced a smile. 'Four months' rent.'

Simmons studied him, a bemused look on his face. 'I'm sorry, but I don't know you.'

'I'm here on someone's behalf.'

'And whom might that be?'

'Nia Mason.'

'Nia Mason?'

'She rents Garreg cottage.'

Simmons stopped smiling. 'Oh, you mean Mrs Haines?'

Flynn stared at him. He didn't like Simmons. He reminded him of his solicitor. It was the pinstriped suit perhaps, or the salmon pink shirt with the gold cufflinks. He also disliked the way he leaned back into his chair and the misguided certainty in his voice. Flynn considered giving him a slap but restrained himself, concluding he'd keep that pleasure until later.

'It's all there,' Flynn said. 'I can wait while you count it.'

Simmons placed a finger on his lips and then rested it on his chin. 'Hmm, you know you could have paid this into the bank. The money's taken automatically.'

Flynn leaned forward in his chair. 'Yeah, Nia mentioned that, but I wanted to see you.'

Simmons's face paled. 'I'll write you a receipt if you'll bear with me.'

He plucked a pen from his inside pocket, then removed his receipt book from a pile of papers. He scribbled something down, mumbling to himself. 'You said you brought four months' rent?'

Flynn nodded. 'Yeah, why?'

Simmons looked up. 'It's better than nothing, I suppose.'

'What d'you mean?'

Simmons leaned back into his chair and placed his hands behind his head. 'Well, she's in arrears for six.'

'*Six*? She told me it was two.'

'I can't comment on that. All I know is they have paid no rent since they moved in.'

'But you let them stay there.'

'I gave them the benefit of the doubt, Mr?'

'Flynn.'

'Especially after Mr Haines's accident.'

Flynn placed his hands on the desk. 'I was told you tried for a little while but became impatient.'

Simmons sat up and folded his arms across his chest. 'I've been more than reasonable, Mr Flynn. I've tried to speak with Mrs Haines on several occasions. I've had nothing but abuse; she has quite a mouth on her.'

Flynn glared at him. 'It seems you've got a lot to say too.'

They sat in silence. Simmons shuffled his papers and glanced at the door.

Flynn got up. 'I'll get the rest of the money for you, but I need more time.'

Simmons nodded. 'Yes,' falling silent as Flynn leaned closer.

'And keep your mouth shut about Nia,' Flynn said. 'I don't like the way you talk about her. If I hear you saying anything else about her, I'll be doing more than knocking on your door.'

18

Simmons's words stayed with Flynn through the alleyways and streets. They sliced him like the rain, bleeding into his skin. He'd half a mind to go back there and show the man who he was dealing with. He thought better of it. For now, the fear in Simmons's eyes was enough. He turned up his collar and continued walking, stopping when he reached Whiteley's store. He stepped inside, grabbed a basket and started browsing along the aisles. He filled it with everything that took his fancy: a loaf of bread, biscuits, tins of beans, and soup.

The woman behind the counter flashed him a dirty smile. She leaned over and started taking the items from the basket. 'Let me scan these in for you,' she said, her hand brushing against his.

He guessed she was in her mid to late forties. She'd a splendid figure. A little top-heavy perhaps, and her dyed brown hair was greying at the roots. Her nails were long and varnished, and a large diamond ring glinted on her finger. He imagined she'd be willing to please her man in bed, at least until she grew bored with him.

She caught him staring but didn't seem to mind. 'Are you here on your holidays?'

Flynn nodded and looked towards the door behind the counter. It opened into a small room, stacked with boxes. A man rested on his haunches, part of his face glowing beneath the fluorescent light. He wore blue overalls, mumbling to himself as he scribbled on a piece of paper.

The woman raised her eyes. 'That's my Dougie. He spends most of his life in that storeroom. God knows what he gets up to.'

Flynn strained a smile and gathered up his shopping.

'Do you want a bag, love?'

He nodded, this time, brushing her hand with his.

Her eyes fixed on his, and her face looked a little flushed. 'That's £7.80 please,' she said.

He handed her a twenty, eyeing her shape as she put it in the till.

'I haven't seen you around here before,' she said. 'What made you come here for your holidays?'

'I'm not on my holidays.'

'Oh, are you working around here then? Where are you staying?'

Flynn smiled to himself, amused by her persistence. 'Garreg Cottage, I'm staying with a friend, Nia . . .'

The woman stopped smiling and slammed his change down on the counter. 'Dougie, Dougie, can you come here a minute?'

Dougie sighed. He stood up, turned around and slumped against the door. 'What's the matter now, Jayne? I'm trying to get this done.'

Jayne glared at Flynn. 'This man's staying at Garreg Cottage, with Nia Haines.'

Dougie straightened. 'Is that right?'

Flynn nodded. 'Yeah, not that it's any of your business.'

Jayne glanced at her husband. 'Nia used to be your friend didn't she, Dougie?'

Dougie blushed. 'The thing is Nia, Mrs Haines, owes us quite a lot of money.'

'Is that right,' Flynn said, 'and how much is that?'

Dougie glanced down at the floor, then turned to face his wife.

Jayne folded her arms. 'It's at least two hundred.'

Flynn took out his wallet and flicked through the notes. 'Here you go,' he said, slamming the cash down on the counter.

Dougie took a deep breath and forced a smile. 'This is all very embarrassing.'

Jayne grabbed the money and counted it. 'It's only what she owes us. Nia Haines doesn't get embarrassed that easily.'

'What's that supposed to mean?' Flynn said.

Dougie walked over to the counter. 'Nothing; take no notice of her. Jayne gets a bit carried away sometimes.'

Jayne glared at her husband. '*I* get carried away. You're a right one to talk. I think you're confusing me with someone else.'

Dougie rubbed a hand across the back of his neck. 'Just be quiet, Jayne.'

'No, I won't. I'm not the one throwing myself at every man in the street, pretending to be a woman of God while spending all night in the pub.'

'Nia doesn't drink,' Flynn said.

Jayne forced a laugh. 'Oh, is that what she told you. He sounds like you, Dougie; you were always taken in by her.'

'Shut it, Jayne,' Dougie said, and he and Flynn exchanged a glance.

Flynn sighed, picked up his shopping, and walked towards the door. He could feel Jayne's eyes burn into him.

'And don't come here again,' she shouted.

Flynn turned around. His fists clenched. 'Don't worry, I've no intention to.' He glanced at Dougie, thinking how pathetic he looked; he fixed Jayne with a stare. 'Do you have no sympathy for her at all, especially after what she's been through?'

A defiant look settled in Jayne's eyes. 'And what's that exactly?'

Flynn shook his head. 'Losing her partner.'

Jayne grinned. 'She seems all right to me. Anyway, she has you now doesn't she, paying her debts, taking *good care* of her.'

19

As Flynn strode down the street, he cursed Simmons, Dougie and Jayne, and anybody he saw. Nothing surprised him. He'd seen it all before, the gossip, jealousy, the spitefulness and resentment. What else could you expect from this arse of the world? The place wasn't even a town. That's why he could never settle, always moving from place to place. But things were different now, and he had Nia to thank for that. Once he'd taken care of his mother, he'd settle down. All those crazy days were long behind him. He liked the idea of being a husband and a dad, and as his mother kept saying, *a person needs to feel grounded.*

It was getting dark, the rain and mist conniving with the dwindling light. A cold dampness slithered over him, causing him to break into a jog. He ran for a few minutes, then stood outside the White Lion, the air's beery smell enticing him in. What harm could it do? It'd been a bad day. A few short whiskies couldn't hurt anyone.

20

It was almost ten when Flynn got back. By the expression on her face, Nia could smell the drink on him. But to her credit, she didn't say a thing. She just sat with him on the sofa, listening to the crackling fire.

'You're quiet,' she said. 'You haven't said a word since you got back.'

'I paid Simmons some rent, although you owe a lot more than you said.'

She glanced down at the carpet. 'I wasn't sure how much it was, to be honest. Martin always dealt with that stuff.'

Flynn sighed. 'I got the impression Simmons felt hard done by.'

She let go of his hand. 'Why? What did he say?'

'Nothing much, only that he tried to be reasonable, but you gave him a mouthful.'

She sat up. 'He was rude to me, Ned. I don't take crap from anyone, let alone *him*.'

Flynn nodded. 'Yeah, he seemed sure of himself. I just wish you would have told me.'

'Well, you know now,' she said. She moved closer, pressed against him, and looked into his eyes. He feared what she saw there, a lover's anguish, or just another smitten fool. He sighed.

'What's wrong?' she said.

'Nothing.'

She kissed him on the cheek. 'Yes, there is. You've got that look about you.'

'What look?'

'Like a little boy lost. Come on; tell me what's bothering you?'

'I had a bit of trouble in Whiteley's store.'

Nia stroked her throat. 'What happened?'

'I paid off your debt.'

'And?'

'I had a row with the owner.'

Nia smiled to herself. 'Jayne Whiteley, now there's a woman with a mouth on her.'

'She seemed to imply–'

'What? That I'd slept with every man in the village?' She stood up. 'Her husband kept coming onto *me*. She seems to think I encouraged it. What else did she say?'

'Something about you always being in the pub.'

'I went for one drink, after Martin's accident. I wanted to be around people for a while. I think that's understandable considering.' She fixed him with a stare. 'You believe me, don't you? Don't let her get to you. This place twists everything. You take too much notice sometimes. Your imagination works overtime, especially when you've been...'

'Been what?'

'Drinking.'

Before he could respond she knelt in front of him and

smoothed her hands across his thighs. He couldn't take his eyes off her. Her collarbone shone beneath the lights, and her dress clung to her like a second skin.

21

Nia went walking every morning. Sometimes, Flynn followed her, keeping his distance as she ambled along the shore. It was like watching a ghost, a pale shadow dissolving in and out of sight. She always kept close to the water's edge, as though taunting the waves as they opened out onto the sand. The cruel winds never deterred her; neither did the rain or the cold. She told him once that the sand seemed to whistle beneath her feet.

'It's a haunting sound,' she said, 'almost like death's whisper.'

22

'I recognise you now, Flynn,' Bevan said, as they unloaded the Land Rover.

Flynn said nothing. He just carried on walking, the sack of logs digging into his shoulder. He emptied it onto the grass, filling the air with the scent of chopped wood. He wiped the sawdust from his clothes and leaned against the shed. He rolled himself a cigarette, watching Bevan struggle with the last sack.

Bevan dragged it across the grass, sitting on top of it as he tried to catch his breath. 'Damn thing,' he said, 'those logs will be the death of me.' He lit a cigarette, closing his eyes as he took a hard drag. A small cloud of smoke drifted above the grass, withering as it settled across the trees.

'Liverpool Stadium,' Bevan said.

Flynn narrowed his eyes. 'What about it?'

'That's where I remember you from. I saw you fight.'

Flynn smiled to himself. 'I was just a kid then; it was a long time ago.'

'True, and you've filled out a lot since; you were a welterweight as far as I remember.' Bevan rubbed his chin. 'You fought Billy Briers. He knocked you about a bit.'

Flynn nodded. 'Yeah, he did, till I put him down in the fifth.'

Bevan laughed. 'You had lovely timing, Flynn. It's a shame about all that trouble you got into.'

'And how would you know about that?'

'I remember hearing about it.'

'Most of that was the drink, but it was a long time ago.'

Bevan nodded. 'Aye, I suppose you're right. You've got yourself a nice girl now; it never pays to dwell on the past.'

Bevan held his cigarette in front of his mouth, the smoke curling through his fingers. 'You know I didn't care much for you, at first, thought you were rough. But you're all right, Flynn. You're far better than Haines ever was.'

'What makes you say that?'

'What you see is what you get. People know where they are with you. There's a kindness in your soul. You don't need to look too hard to see that.' Bevan drew on his cigarette. 'Haines was a schemer. He was a destructive influence on Nia, brought her nothing but trouble, even when he was dead.'

'How d'you mean?'

'He left her with nothing, just a load of debts, and a useless insurance policy. But I don't need to tell you about Haines, you knew what he was like.'

'No, I don't. I've only seen him once, well kind of.'

'What do you mean *kind of*?'

'The first night I came here, I thought I saw him in the woods.'

Bevan gave him a long look and then stood up. 'What are you talking about? Haines was long gone by then, probably someone else.' Bevan shook his head and laughed. 'I think you've had too many knocks on the head. Dead men don't go wandering in the woods. This place doesn't have any ghosts.'

'You should tell Nia that.'

'What d'you mean?'

'She's always praying for him. She's even got a special room, spends hours in there.'

'Doing what exactly?'

Flynn shrugged. 'I don't know. She won't let me go in there. Then she goes on those walks, every morning. I follow her sometimes. It's as though she's searching for him across the sands.'

Bevan rested a hand on Flynn's shoulder. 'She just needs time, and you need to get out more. Don't think like this. A man needn't be jealous of the dead.'

23

That morning, as was her routine, Nia got up at dawn. Flynn pretended to be asleep, listening to the rain pattering against the window. The minute she left the house, he scrambled out of bed. He chose not to follow her; instead, he searched the house for a picture of Haines to put his mind at rest.

He foraged through drawers and cabinets, sifting through junk mail, unpaid bills, and bundles of scribbled notes. Beneath a stack of newspapers, he discovered an old shoebox. He dragged it out and flipped off the lid, then took out a heap of photographs. Most of the pictures were of Nia. She looked so young, barely out of her teens. In one of them, she leaned against a garden fence, holding a puppy. The dog's doleful eyes stared up at her, but Nia seemed indifferent. Instead, she smiled into the camera, holding the puppy as though it was a hindrance.

Flynn browsed through the remaining photographs, growing more dissatisfied. The one he wanted to see wasn't there. He threw them onto the floor, stood up, and made his way upstairs. He went into Nia's room, searching the cupboards and drawers until he found more photographs. To his surprise, there were no photographs of Haines. She must have had some. Where the hell did she keep them? Then it came to him, and he hurried across the landing to her special room.

Even though the door was locked, Flynn kept pressing down on the handle. When it didn't budge, he rammed it with his shoulder, splitting the wood and snapping it at the hinges. He lurched forward, almost falling onto the carpet. The room was dark, painted black, with wooden blinds behind the curtains. He glimpsed candles huddled around a mirror, and above them, hanging on the wall, was a painting of the Virgin Mary.

Before he stepped inside, he turned around, sensing someone behind him.

Nia glared at him. 'What the hell are you doing? You've no right to be in here.'

'I was looking for something; I couldn't find the key. So I–'

'So, you kicked the door down? What the hell are you playing at?'

Flynn's eyes met hers. 'I've been meaning to ask you the same thing.'

'This is my house, Ned.'

'Yeah, I know, and if you haven't noticed, I'm living in it, too.'

'Well, you can always leave if you don't like it.'

'Is that what you want?'

She turned her back on him and made her way across the landing. He chased after her, grabbed her arms and turned her towards him. 'Don't turn your back on me. I asked you a question.'

'You're hurting me, Ned.'

He let go of her and took a step back. 'I'm sick of it; any man would be.'

She made her way downstairs. Flynn followed her, watching as she gazed at the upturned drawers, her eyes fixing on the shoebox on the floor.

'I'm sorry about the mess,' he said. 'I'll clean it up.'

'What were you looking for?'

'A photograph.'

'Of who?'

'Haines.'

'What for?'

'See what he looked like.'

She sighed and walked over to the window. 'You won't find any. I burned most of them. Don't ask me why. I just did.'

He knelt and began picking up the papers, piling them into a stack before shoving them in the drawer. He sensed Nia watching him, felt her eyes scanning him with disapproval. 'I'll borrow some tools,' he said.

'What for?'

'The bedroom door.'

'Don't bother, just fetch Bevan, ask him to fix it.'

'I can do it myself.'

'I want Bevan to do it. I don't want you going near there. You've done enough damage for one day.'

While Bevan fixed the door, Flynn waited outside, smoking in the garden. The cold midday air nipped at his fingers. He kept watching the house, then threw down his cigarette as Nia opened the front door. She walked towards him, holding something. There was no expression on her face as she offered him the photograph. 'Go on,' she said, 'take it.'

'Listen, I–'

'What's your problem, Ned? Come on, I thought you wanted to know what he looks like.'

Flynn sheepishly accepted the photograph and stared down at it. He brushed a hand over his mouth, struggling to shield his surprise. The picture showed Nia and Haines leaning against a tree. The sun hung low. Rays of light sifted through the branches. Nia was beaming, and it was the happiest he'd ever seen her. Haines was tall and broad, his dark eyes staring back at Flynn, giving him that same spiteful look, the one he'd seen in the woods.

'What the hell's wrong with you?' Nia said.

Flynn didn't respond; his heart pounding as he let the photograph slip through his fingers.

24

Nia had ignored him since early morning, shoving him away whenever he tried to make amends. Flynn spent the rest of the afternoon pacing the room, watching the clock, or staring out of the window. They didn't talk until later that evening, when Flynn asked, 'How long are you going to be like this? It's driving me crazy.'

'I'm sorry,' she sighed, and placed her arms around his waist.

Flynn inhaled her perfume, closed his eyes, savouring her warm skin.

'What are we going to do, Ned?'

He squeezed her hand. 'We're all right. It was my fault, rushing about like a maniac. I don't know what's wrong with me. I had no right to be in there.'

He turned her towards him, took hold of her face, and kissed her gently. 'We're going to be fine. From now on, there'll be no more arguments.'

She gave him the hint of a smile, the gleam in her eyes melting. 'I'm not talking about arguments or that stupid door. How are we going to live, buy food, pay the rent?'

Flynn dug his hands into his pockets, feeling the sharp edges of his last few notes. His stomach rumbled, and he was almost out of cigarettes. 'We'll be fine. I still have a few hundred left. Then I'll get some work; I'm sure Bevan can find me something.'

Nia moved away from him, sat down on the sofa, and stared into the dying fire.

Flynn knelt in front of her. 'Stop worrying, I promise you, I'll find something.'

She smiled at him, almost as though he were a child. 'There's no work here, Ned. It's late autumn; everything's out of season.'

He stood up. 'We'll go somewhere else then. There's nothing to keep us here, not the way they've treated you.'

'And where will we go? At least we've got a roof over our heads. Well, for a month.'

'We can stay at my mother's. She'd like that. She sure as hell could do with the company.' Flynn pictured the sadness in his mother's eyes. He felt a sudden bout of shame, and without thinking said, 'that's the only reason I took this job.'

'You can always go back, you know.'

'We both can.'

'No. Not with Mason still there. He'd make my life hell if I ever went back to that place.' She slid her hands down her face, resting them on her throat. 'We'd be fine if just paid what he owes me.'

Flynn sat beside her. 'What d'you mean?'

'What did he tell you about that letter I sent him?'

Flynn shrugged. 'Only what I've told you; he said you needed money. That you'd gotten yourself into a mess.'

'Did he show you the letter?'

Flynn shook his head.

'I didn't beg him for money, Ned. I just asked him for what he owed me. That's why he sent you, to fetch me back, to shut me up.'

Flynn nodded. 'How much does he owe you?'

'Twenty-thousand at least, but I would have settled for ten.'

Flynn laughed. '*Twenty-thousand*. How come he owes you that much?'

'It's my share of the business, contracts I tendered for, deals I closed and brokered.'

'I didn't realise you were such a businesswoman.'

'I'm not lying to you, Ned. And don't mock me. I practically ran the place.'

'So why did you run off then?'

She rested her head against his shoulder. 'Mason went crazy when he found out about Martin and me. You know what he's like. God knows what he might have done.'

Flynn leaned forward.

'What's the matter?' she said.

'Haines... I don't like you mentioning him.'

'I can't just forget about him. He was a big influence on my life.'

'Yeah, a bad one, so I've heard.'

'I never thought I'd hear that kind of talk from you.'

'Why?'

'You know what it's like, people giving you a bad reputation, distorting every story.'

Flynn stared down at his hands, at the scars, the broken finger, and the hard patches of skin. 'Twenty-thousand,' he whispered.

'I know,' Nia said. 'If that tight-fisted, old bastard paid

up, it would solve all our problems. I'd give you a cut, Ned, and help your mother out too.'

Flynn fixed her with a stare. 'Do you mean that?'

'Of course, I do.'

'I better see him then. Perhaps it's time to call in the debt.'

'What if he refuses to pay?'

'Oh, he will.'

'What makes you so sure?'

'I'll persuade him.'

PART II

IN THE QUIETNESS BEFORE THE GRAVE

1

Flynn travelled by train, late in the evening, catching glimpses of moonlight spilling across the bay. Much to his relief, the carriage was virtually empty, and he savoured the half-silence. He slid into his seat, thinking of Nia, observing the soft outline of his shadow beneath the fluorescent lights. She was all he needed. All he'd ever wanted. Such thoughts made him feel selfish, and as he pictured his mother, he grew more determined to make things right.

Flynn shut his eyes, and amid the tireless chug of the train remembered what Nia said.

'Don't let Mason convince you he keeps no money in the house. He's got it stashed everywhere. Money boxes in the lounge and in the study there's a safe.'

She scribbled the combination and handed him the slip of paper. *'He owes us, Ned. Don't let him try to tell you otherwise. Don't let him mess with your head. Please, don't take no for an answer. Promise me, Ned.'*

2

Empty train stations were the loneliest of places, as were the grey dishevelled buildings, and the silent, rain-drenched streets. Flynn avoided the town, keeping his head bowed as he drifted through the avenues. He paused opposite his mother's house, keeping his distance, staring at the living room window. A tear of light cut through the curtains, but except for that, the place looked deserted. He was desperate to see how she was but couldn't risk it; she'd never been one for keeping secrets. If things went to plan, he'd visit her on his way back, stay with her for a few days; get her that help she needed. Not that she ever complained. He could do no wrong in her eyes. She wouldn't have a word said against him. He pictured himself as a boy, sat on her lap, his head resting on her shoulder.

'You've got a soft heart, Ned,' she'd whispered, 'don't let it be the ruin of you.'

Flynn took a deep breath and carried on walking. He took a shortcut through the meadows. The wind moaned through the trees, and the grass was slick beneath his feet. He sniffed the air as a cloud of blue smoke wafted above the fields. He caught sight of the chimney first, and then the huge white house; its lighted windows shone through the neighbouring woods.

Flynn crouched down, aware of his every breath. He started making his way through the darkness, wet blades of grass slicing across his skin. As he approached the house, he hesitated, his eyes flitting from window to window. Mason's Jag stood in the drive, the bonnet gleaming beneath the outside light.

Flynn kept his head down, following the fence until he reached the back of the house. He climbed into the garden, then started crawling through the grass, conscious of the backpack on his shoulders. He sneaked up the patio steps, watching, waiting.

Satisfied it was all clear, he sidled across the flagstones, keeping his back to the wall. When he reached the doors, he turned the handle. As expected, it was locked. He slipped a hand into his coat and pulled out a metal tube, then placed it over the cylinder, driving it back and forth until he felt something click. A dog yapped in the distance, and for a minute, Flynn stood paralysed. He slipped the bar back into his coat, took out a screwdriver, and kept prodding the cylinder until he heard it clatter to the floor. Then he pressed it into the lock, twisting and turning it until the door swung open.

The clouds had broken now, and moonlight splashed across the floor. Flynn looked around the room, at the porcelain figurines, the leather chairs, and the antique tables. Everything looked so clean, untouched. A woman's portrait watched him from the wall, her eyes following him as he stepped into the hallway. Flynn crept upstairs, following the hissing of Mason's chest into the bedroom. Mason lay fast asleep, like a child, swathed in a large quilt.

The old man murmured something. Then his eyes opened, widening with fear as Flynn put his hand across his mouth.

Mason struggled at first until Flynn pressed harder.

'Keep still,' Flynn said, 'don't make things hard for yourself.'

Mason nodded, and Flynn removed his hand.

The old man pushed himself up from the bed, his spindly arms trembling. 'What's all this about?'

Flynn pointed to the door. 'Come on, get up.'

Mason sighed and put on his dressing-gown. He plodded across the carpet, squinting when Flynn switched on the light.

Flynn shoved him towards the landing. 'Come on, hurry, I haven't got all night.'

Mason made his way downstairs, Flynn walking behind him. They said nothing as they walked into the room, as though still unsure of each other like on the first day they met. Flynn nodded at the desk. 'How much money do you have in there?'

Mason shrugged. 'Not much, a grand at the most.'

Flynn gave him another shove. 'Fetch it then and put it over there.'

Mason took the money from the drawer and slammed it on the table. 'What the hell are you playing at, Flynn? I thought we had a deal?'

Flynn slipped the backpack off his shoulders, rested it on the table, and put the money inside. Then he walked over to the fireplace and lifted the painting off the wall.

'Open the safe,' Flynn said.

Mason shook his head. 'Sorry, I can't do that.'

Flynn reached into his trouser pocket and pulled out a slip of paper. 'No problem, I'll just have to do it myself then.'

He keyed in the numbers, grinning as the safe opened.

Flynn stared at the packs of notes, the diamond rings, and the gold bracelets.

Mason grabbed Flynn's arm, squeezing it hard as though his life depended on it. 'You won't get away with this, Flynn. I'll send people to find you.'

Flynn brushed Mason's hand away and emptied the contents of the safe into the backpack. 'What people? All I see is a tired old man, alone in an empty house.'

'You're wrong to think that.'

Flynn pushed him aside. 'I'm only taking what's owed to her. It's not as if I'm bleeding you dry, from what Nia tells me you've got plenty in the bank.'

Hatred filled the old man's eyes. 'She's playing you for a fool, got you right where she wants you.'

'That makes two of you then; only she's a better prospect.'

Mason shook his head. 'Is that right, and what about Haines, where does he fit into all this?'

Flynn felt a lump in his throat. 'He doesn't; he died months ago.'

Mason fell silent, then said, 'And you're sure about that?'

'What d'you mean?'

'That girl's a born liar, she probably made it up.'

Flynn pushed his face closer. 'You sick old fool. Why would she lie about something like that?'

'Because that's what she does; you don't know her like I do.'

'So why are you so desperate to get her back?'

Mason grinned. 'I thought you'd know that by now. There's only one thing she's good for.'

Flynn grabbed Mason's shoulders and forced him against the wall. 'Just keep your nasty mouth shut.'

The old man's eyes lightened. 'There's no need to be like that, Ned. I'm only trying to do you a favour.'

'Is that right?' Flynn said and stepped away from him. He watched the old man in silence, the room growing colder. Mason was messing with his head, just as Nia had warned him. He didn't have to listen to this. All he had to do was walk away. But the old man kept taunting him, his words like an unreachable itch, teasing at the back of his mouth. He pictured Haines that night in the woods, peering at him through the trees.

Mason smoothed the creases from his gown. 'You've got your doubts, though. I can tell that just by looking at you.'

Flynn sighed; sweat tickled down his neck. He watched Mason walk over to the drinks cabinet and take out a bottle of whisky. He poured some into a glass and offered it to Flynn.

Flynn shook his head, then watched Mason take a sip.

'You're missing out,' Mason said. 'This is a Glenn Gran '48.'

Flynn licked his lips. 'No thanks. I'm trying to keep away from it.' Mason nodded. 'Sorry, I forgot. This stuff brings out the worst in you.'

Flynn ignored the dig, grabbed the backpack, and motioned towards the door. The old man blocked his way. 'I meant what I said, Flynn, about finding you.'

Flynn laughed. 'That won't be hard will it; you know where I've been for the last month.'

Mason pushed his face closer. 'And I know what you've been doing too.'

The rain hammered against the windows, the shadows fading as the sky darkened. Flynn glanced about the room, unsettled by its eerie silence. He knew exactly how Mason felt, those niggling doubts, and the jealousy that brooded inside him. 'She's never coming back, you know,' Flynn said, the softness of his own voice surprising him.

Mason smiled. 'Don't be so sure. You've no idea what she's capable of.'

The words got under Flynn's skin, like a toxin, stirring up his blood. 'What d'you mean?'

'Nia's a survivor; she does what she needs to.'

'What, like marrying men like you?'

'Yes, men like me, chancers like Haines, and idiots like you.'

Flynn slung the backpack over his shoulder. 'At least I'll be a happy idiot.'

Mason narrowed his eyes. 'I'm curious . . .'

'About what?'

'Why Nia believes that money's hers, what story she's told you.'

'It's like I told you before, she just wants what's owed to her for all the work she's done.'

'What work?' Mason scoffed. 'I suppose doing sweet FA could be regarded as a full-time occupation.'

'I don't believe that. From what Nia tells me, she practically ran your business.'

Mason forced a laugh, almost choking. He cleared his throat. 'You're more stupid than I thought, Flynn. Why don't you try to be smart for once, stop thinking with your dick?'

'Nia said you'd be like this.'

'Like *what*?'

'Full of lies, full of poison.'

Mason gritted his teeth. 'Let me tell you about that precious Nia of yours. You and Haines aren't the first, and you definitely won't be the last.'

Flynn pushed past him and walked into the hall. Mason chased after him, wheezing. He grabbed Flynn's arm and turned him around. 'Don't you dare walk away from me; I haven't finished with you yet.'

Mason looked old, the glare of the hall lights revealing every line and crack. Flynn shoved him aside, but Mason kept on at him, poking and prodding. 'And what's your mother going to say when I tell her about this.'

Flynn grabbed Mason's arms, lifting him as though he were a doll. 'You stay away from my mother; do you hear me.'

Mason grinned. 'Just being a good neighbour, Flynn. She deserves to know what her son's up to. God knows how she'll take it. She might do something daft. Shame does that to people. It might be the finish of her.'

Flynn hurled him across the floor, the old man's head snapping against the wall. Mason stayed on the floor, sprawled in his own blood.

'Get up,' Flynn said. 'Come on, stop acting.'

But Mason didn't move, even when Flynn gave him a nudge.

3

Flynn sat alone in the half-empty carriage, drinking Mason's Glenn Gran '48. It had a peaty bite to it, other than that it was nothing special, just another bottle of whisky. Its heady aroma lingered as he gazed through the window, listening to the muffled sound of voices, observing the intermittent flashes of light. The train picked up speed, charging into the dawn. Flynn took another swig, savouring the taste as it burned into his chest. Like everything else these last few weeks, the morning had sneaked up on him; the dawn sun bled through the clouds, colouring the fields with smears of bloodied light. Flynn yawned, refusing to close his eyes for fear of what he might see.

4

When he arrived at the village, Flynn staggered through the cobbled streets, the intense glow of the streetlights dazzling him as he pursued the muffled sound of laughter.

On reaching the White Lion, he looked up at the sign. The beast's fierce glare drew him in. He stepped inside, the warmth from the fire burst across his face.

The barman smiled. 'What can I get you?' he said, looking downwards when Flynn just stared at him.

Somehow Flynn ordered a drink, guzzling it as though it were his last. 'Another pint and a whisky chaser,' he said, slapping his money onto the bar.

Flynn took his drink and teetered over to a table, dropping into a chair, his eyes flitting from face to face. Mason's hatred lingered in every stranger's eyes and his scorn in every woman's smile. Flynn rubbed his hands down his face, his head throbbing to the roar of laughter. The drink took a firmer hold, and he shut his eyes against it.

'Are you all right?' someone said, and an icy hand rested

on Flynn's shoulder. When Flynn opened his eyes, he saw Bevan standing over him.

Bevan shook his head. 'What the hell do you think you're doing? Look at the state of you.'

'Get a round in,' Flynn shouted and slammed a twenty-pound note on the table.

Bevan pulled out a chair and sat next to him. 'No, that's not a good idea. You've had enough.' He studied Flynn for a minute. 'What's wrong?'

Flynn mumbled something. Then stared ahead, his eyes locked on something, as though someone was watching him.

Bevan kept on at him. 'Are you listening to me, Flynn? What the hell are you playing at? Nia's been worried sick.'

Flynn's face relaxed at the mention of her name. Then his expression altered as though absorbed by something darker. 'She still loves him,' he said, closing his eyes at the thought of it.

Bevan grabbed Flynn's arm. 'Come on, let's get you home.'

Flynn pulled away, toppling his pint from the table. The glass smashed onto the floor, and the room fell silent.

'What the hell are you all looking at?' Flynn shouted.

The barman stepped out from behind the bar and walked towards him. 'There's no need to be so aggressive,' he said and started cleaning up the glass.

Flynn banged his fist on the table. 'I'll be what I like.' He stood up and stared at the floor, tried to say something, but struggled to get his words out. Flynn stepped forward, leaning into Bevan as he tried to steady himself. Bevan held onto him. 'Come on, Flynn, it's time we were leaving.'

Flynn looked around the room, every stranger turning when he caught their glance.

'Where is she?' he shouted, the faint sound of laughter following him through the door.

5

Flynn's head throbbed. A dull ache gnawed at his bones as he shuddered against the cold. An emptiness filled his stomach and the raw taste of bile burned across his throat. The pictures came rushing back, and it made no difference whether his eyes were open or shut. He still saw that big white house, the moon, the shadows, and the emptiness in Mason's eyes. They'd find the old man soon enough. It was just a matter of time.

As he gathered his senses, Flynn became aware that he was lying down, fully dressed, in a stranger's bed. Except for a wardrobe in the corner, the room was bare. The air was stifling. The smell of whisky and cigarettes lingered like a terrible memory. He motioned to get up, but the pain in his head kept him grounded. He lay quietly, his heart thumping against that familiar, oppressive silence. Flynn had grown to despise such isolation. A ceaseless hush that so many claimed was tranquillity. The soft sound of the waves, washing across the sands, failed to calm him.

Flynn pulled away the quilt and jumped out of bed. He walked over to the wardrobe, opened it, and peered inside.

All he discovered was an old blanket, and two dubiously stained, pillows. He looked down at them as though waiting for something to appear, eventually slamming the wardrobe door, and then lowering himself onto his knees.

Crawling on all fours, Flynn eased himself onto his stomach. Saliva filled his mouth, his body weakening, and a sudden sickness gripped him. He exhaled deeply and peeped under the bed. There was nothing there but dust, a crushed cigarette packet, and an empty bottle of wine. Flynn rolled onto his back and looked up at the ceiling, studying a fly trapped in a web, defenceless, as a huge spider approached it on an invisible thread. Flynn let out a deep sigh, and using all his strength, pushed himself up. He searched the room, opening and shutting the wardrobe door.

'Where the hell is it?' he shouted, lifting the mattress off the bed and heaving it onto the carpet.

When the bedroom door juddered open, Flynn turned towards it. He remained motionless, watching Bevan tutting at him from the doorway. 'What's all the commotion?' Bevan glanced at the mattress on the carpet. 'Jesus, Flynn, what the hell do you think you're up to?'

'Where's my backpack? I had it with me last night.'

Bevan nodded at Flynn's coat hanging on the door. 'You hung it behind your coat, wouldn't let it out of your sight. Got quite aggressive whenever I got near it.'

Flynn pushed past him and grabbed his coat off the hook. To his relief, the backpack was unopened, the cord still fastened into a knot. He took it off the hook, then went downstairs and sat on the bottom step. Resting the backpack on his knees, Flynn untied the cord and drew it open. The money and jewellery remained exactly how he'd left them. He hadn't counted it yet, but his guess was that there must have been fifty grand there at least. A condemned man's spoils, yet the voice inside his head assured him it was worth it. They'd dreamed of this chance, and for the first time in his life, Flynn was the harbinger of good news. He glanced over his shoulder and saw Bevan watching him from the landing.

'Is everything still there?' Bevan said, an offended tone to his voice.

Flynn nodded.

Bevan walked towards him, pausing halfway down the stairs. 'What the hell have you got in there, anyway?'

Flynn didn't respond, the look in his eyes telling Bevan to mind his own business. He closed the backpack, clutching it tighter as Bevan shuffled past him. The two men kept silent, until Bevan said, 'I'll fix us some breakfast.'

Flynn stood. 'Nah, not for me, I've got too much to do.' He scanned the hall. 'Where are my boots?'

Bevan nodded to where Flynn had left them. 'What's so urgent that you can't have anything to eat?'

'Business. Breakfast can wait. I haven't got the stomach for it.'

Bevan smiled. 'I'm not surprised after knocking back all that drink. You want to stay clear of that stuff. You were speaking like a mad man.'

Flynn put his boots on. 'Why? What did I say?'

Bevan shrugged. 'Who knows? Most of it was unintelligible.' He cast Flynn a glance. 'I'd keep away from the pubs for a while, though.'

'Why's that?'

'Bad news travels fast. I doubt if anyone would serve you.'

Flynn lowered his eyes. 'I'd no intention of going there. Last night was a one-off. I've had my fill of drink.'

'Good, let's hope that remains true.'

Flynn fixed Bevan with a stare. 'Why should you care, anyway?'

'It makes no odds to me what you do. It's Nia I'm worried about.'

'Nia will be fine, don't you worry. I'll see to that, although if push comes to shove, I'm sure she can take care of herself.'

'Push comes to shove, what d'you mean? What are you planning to do?'

'I'm not planning to do anything. It's just a figure of speech.'

Flynn motioned towards the door, causing Bevan to step aside. He felt Bevan's eyes burn into him. The thought of it needled him, as did the incessant tick of the clock. He opened the door, hesitating on the step as he glanced over his shoulder. 'Is that old shovel still by the shed?'

Bevan nodded.

'Can I use it?'

Bevan didn't answer, so Flynn read his silence as a yes. He made his way over to the shed, picked up the shovel and rested it against his shoulder.

'Thanks for helping me last night,' he said, and strode out onto the muddy track.

6

Flynn followed the path for about half a mile until it veered off onto the country lanes. He stamped the mud from his boots and headed for the woods. Sauntering, his body remained weak. A slow ache throbbed inside his head; last night's drink sloshed around in his guts. He foraged in his pocket for a cigarette, changing his mind as a sniff of tobacco made him retch. An engine purred in the distance, provoking him to walk closer to the hedge. The fields beyond were desolate. Rooks scavenged among the meadow, each piercing squawk stressing the uncanny silence. The autumn sky hung low. A weak line of crimson bled across the tips of the trees.

Flynn's hand shook as he wiped the sweat from his brow. The smell of whisky goaded him, as did the image of Mason's face, and the slyness of the old man's smile. Nia wouldn't play him for a fool. He shook his head and moved on, rejecting such notions before any of them could take root.

Whether it was through paranoia or wisdom, the voice in his head told him to bury the backpack–keep it hidden and out of temptation's grasp. As Flynn drew closer to the woods, a sense of dread fell over him. He tried to laugh it off. It was early morning, for God's sake. It would be hours before it turned dark. He took a deep breath, trying to steady himself, inching into the trees, thankful the dreary sky cast no shadows.

Flynn quickened his pace, occasionally stabbing the shovel into the dry earth, using it like a stick. An immediate sense of loneliness seized him as he ventured further into the woods. He felt cut off from everything, the outside world nothing but a murmur, brought in by a cruel breeze. A man could go crazy here, left alone. Flynn stopped and set the backpack on the ground, then removed his jacket and flung it over a branch. He pushed the shovel into the soil, concluding this place was as good as any.

Before he started digging, Flynn carved his mother's initials into a tree. They were hardly noticeable, but enough for him to know. Then he collected some stones, piling them on top of each other a metre or so away from the spot. He spat into his palms then forced the shovel deeper into the soil, digging frantically, striking the earth as though it were the embodiment of all his sorrow.

With each shovelful of soil, Flynn dug faster, feeling better now, sweat oozing from every pore.

Every few minutes, he paused to catch his breath, instantly returning to his task whenever he glimpsed something in the trees. He felt someone watching him, something easing closer. '*Stop acting like a fool,*' he told himself and began digging faster, shovelling the soil into a large pile behind him.

Satisfied the hole was deep enough, Flynn rested the shovel on the ground. He mopped the sweat from his face with his sleeve, leaned over and picked up the backpack. It was better this way. Lay low for a while. Wait until they'd buried Mason. Let time pass. Nia would agree it made sense. And if she didn't, he was positive he'd convince her. Only a fool would spend that money straight away, and a fool was something he no longer wanted to be.

7

Flynn counted the money, the rings, and necklaces, three times before he buried them. Even after they were beneath the ground, he returned to the spot twice to check on it. He felt lighter as he made his way back. Digging that hole had sweated the drink out of him, although the image of Mason's face still hounded him like a terrible memory.

It was midday when he reached the crossroads. A low sun slid through the clouds, sifting through the trees, and mottling the fields with shadow. When he turned up at the cottage, Nia was standing by the window. He paused by the gate and watched her, making his way up the path when she declined to return his smile.

When he walked inside, a drift of cold air met him in the hallway. It pursued him into the lounge, lurking beneath his skin. Flynn rubbed his hands. 'Jesus, this place is freezing.'

Nia nodded at the coal scuffle. 'Do something about it then.'

Flynn resigned himself to his task, knelt in front of the fire, snatched a handful of sticks, and organised them into a square on the grate. Then he split up a firelighter and lay the pieces on top of the sticks, repeating these steps until he'd built a small stack. He lit the pieces of firelighter and watched the flames rising. He'd learned this method as a boy. Every morning before school, he'd watched his mother prepare a fire. Even now, after all these years, he still set the coals on the flames how she'd shown him. The picture of his mother sitting alone in her house refused to leave him. He could almost hear that old clock of hers ticking away the hours. He cast the image aside. It was too risky for him to see her. He'd sort things out soon enough. The kindest thing he could do was to stay away.

Flynn drew away from the fire, shaken by the faces he saw there. He thought about Mason, wondered how long it would be before they found him? Was he still lying there, as lifeless as the furnishings in his home? The things Mason had assembled were of no benefit to him now. That big white house was nothing but a shell, soon to be auctioned off, and doomed to be another rich man's home. Mason's wealth was of no use to him either.

The sound of two cups, clinking down on the table, forced him to his senses. Nia stood in front of him, a sullen look on her face.

'What's your problem?' he said.

'What's *my* problem? Surely, I should ask you. Where have you been? I've been at my wit's end, imagining all kinds of scenarios.'

He glanced down at his hands. 'I had a few drinks, got a little carried away.'

She gave him a questioning look. 'And why the hell were you drinking?'

'There was a problem.'

'Problem? What problem? Ned? Ned, answer me for God's sake.'

He slumped into the sofa, watching as Nia sat next to him.

Flynn leaned forward and picked up a cup, relishing the steam on his face.

Nia gave him a nudge. 'What problem, Ned. Tell me, for Christ's sake.'

He banged the cup down on the table. 'I've got your money if that's what you're concerned about.'

She scowled. 'Did I mention anything about money?'

'No, but that's what you were thinking.'

'I was thinking about you. Where the hell have you been? You look dreadful. What's this problem?'

'Mason...'

'What, he's sent men after you?'

Flynn shook his head.

'What then?'

'There's... There's been an accident.'

She stood up. 'What kind of accident?'

He looked down at the carpet. 'Mason's .... things got a bit out of hand.'

'What's that supposed to mean?'

Flynn stood and wandered over to the window. 'He was harping on about stuff. Badgering me, spreading his filthy lies, making threats about my mother.' He smoothed his hand across the back of his neck. 'Hell, you know more than anyone what he's like.'

'What have you done, Ned?'

He stared through the window. 'I lost my temper, gripped him and shoved him against the wall.'

'Was he hurt? Ned? Ned, answer me for God's sake.'

'He cracked his skull; there was blood everywhere.'

'Jesus, Ned, did you call an ambulance?'

'There was no need. He was dead before he hit the floor.'

'What did you do with him?'

'Nothing.'

'You just left him there?'

'I needed to get away. Don't worry, nobody saw me. I never left a trace.'

She squared up to him, stopping but a breath away. 'What the hell have you done, Ned?'

He wiped the spray of spittle from his face. '*We* did what we had to.'

Her face paled. 'We?'

'Yeah, you're just as much a part of this as I am.'

'And how do you figure that out?'

'It was your idea to go back there. You gave me the combination to the safe.'

'I said nothing about murder.'

'I didn't murder anyone. It was an accident.' He sighed, lowering his voice as he said, 'The last thing we need to do is panic. Don't worry, I was careful.'

Nia grabbed a fistful of her hair, and for a second it looked as though she was about to yank it out from the roots. '*Careful*? He's *dead*, Ned. How the hell is that being careful?'

'It was an accident. I got the money, didn't I? You wouldn't have got a penny out of him otherwise.'

She dropped her hands to her sides and sagged against the wall. 'What good is that money to us now? The police would just use it as evidence.'

'The *police*? Who said anything about them?'

'We can't just leave it like this.'

'Why not, and why should you care? You know more than anyone that the old bastard deserved it.'

'What if someone saw you?'

He shook his head. 'I've been sneaking in and out of houses all my life. Believe me, I was careful.'

They looked at each other for a minute, and then Nia said, 'So what are we supposed to do?'

'Sit it out.'

'For how long?'

'For as long as it takes . . . a few months at the most.'

'But what if they come here?'

'Who?'

'The police, solicitors.'

'And why would they do that?'

She sighed. 'Because I'm probably down as his next of kin.'

Flynn hadn't thought of that, and a sudden feeling of alarm rushed inside him. 'Let's play it by ear then. Take it as it comes. We can deal with anything, as long as we remain calm.'

'And you can manage that?'

He pictured the stranger in the woods, his throat feeling dry as he caught the faint smell of whisky. 'I can manage anything, as long as you're beside me.'

Nia clasped her hands as though bracing herself for prayer. 'I don't know, Ned. All this for ten grand, hardly seems worth it.'

'I wouldn't disagree, but it's not for ten grand. It's a hell of a lot more than that.'

'How much?'

As hard as he tried, he couldn't stop smiling. 'Fifty grand in cash at least and then there's all the jewellery.'

'You took all the rings and necklaces from the safe?'

He nodded.

'Ned, was one of those a sapphire platinum ring?'

Flynn nodded.

'That on its own is worth over two hundred thousand.'

He laughed. 'Good, it's about time we had some luck.'

'Where have you put them?'

'Don't worry about that; they're in a safe place.'

She frowned. 'In a *safe place*?'

'Yeah, where no one else can find them.'

'Where, for Christ's sake?

He smiled to himself. 'Trust me, it's better that you don't know.'

'*Why*? Don't you *trust* me?'

'It's not that. It makes things easier, especially if it all goes tits-up.'

'And what makes you come to that conclusion?'

'Because if we get caught, I won't tell them anything, but we'll still have something to believe in, something to keep us going, keep us together, to come back to years later.'

'You make it sound like we're already caught.'

'I don't mean to. That's just the worst-case scenario.'

'And the best one?'

'That we sit it out, stick together, and before we know it, we'll be away from here.'

'And what about your mother?'

'She's going to be fine. I'll make sure of that.'

8

In the days that followed, Flynn tried hard to keep his demons at bay. For a while, he was successful. They tormented him from a distance. Only creeping into his thoughts when he was tired, or whenever his mind wandered. At night, when they drew closer, he tried to protect himself. He pictured Haines's figure on the sands, swept away by the tide. He kept the image of Mason's body at a distance too, reminding himself that the past was best forgotten.

The shift in the weather gave a brief respite. The wind had drifted east, making the days feel calmer. Flynn had asked Nia to help him. She still went for her walks, but now, on Flynn's insistence, she took another route that avoided the shore. She still prayed. Yet, afterwards, the door to her shrine remained locked.

Everything was running to plan. Flynn even stayed free of the drink. Then, one afternoon, Nia returned home early, storming into the house with a newspaper tucked under her arm.

'What's wrong?' Flynn said.

She handed him the newspaper. 'Here. Have a look for yourself.'

He remained motionless, gripping the paper in his hand.

Through gritted teeth, Nia said, 'Read it; page nine.'

Flynn flicked through the pages, his heart thumping when he looked at the headline: 'MAN'S BODY FOUND IN SUSPICIOUS CIRCUMSTANCES.'

He flung the paper across the room, his hands trembling as the panic set in.

Nia shook her head. 'That's really going to help.'

When he managed to compose himself, Flynn picked up the paper and reread the headline, and this time he read the article too. 'It took them a week to find him,' he said, without glancing up, then dropped the paper onto the sofa and stared at Nia in silence.

'So?' she said.

Flynn shrugged. 'All it says is that the investigation's ongoing.'

'But it made the papers.'

'Only the locals.'

Nia sighed. 'What part of this don't you get? It says suspicious circumstances. They're treating this as murder.'

Flynn folded his arms across his chest. 'I know that, but these investigations take months. You know the people Mason dealt with. There'll be loads of suspects.'

Nia stepped forward. 'But there's the letter. The one I wrote to him, asking for money. It's got my name on it and everything.'

Flynn smiled. 'I wouldn't worry if I were you; I watched him burn it.'

'And the others?'

'What others?'

'The people who know you're here.'

Flynn walked over to the coffee table and picked up his pack of cigarettes. He put one into his mouth, lit it, and took a deep drag, blowing the smoke up at the ceiling. 'Mason didn't tell anyone as far as I know. He warned me to keep it quiet. You know how vain he was. He didn't want anyone finding out that he'd paid someone to fetch his wife back. He'd do anything to save face.'

'Perhaps, but the police will come knocking on my door, eventually.'

'What makes you so sure?'

'I already told you; I'm probably Mason's next of kin.'

Flynn squeezed the tip of his cigarette, almost breaking it. He flicked it into the fire and walked over to the window. Vast clouds floated above the fields, and a wash of sunlight marked the horizon. He turned around and held Nia's stare with his own. 'Nobody even knows you're here.'

'But they will.'

'Take them a while, though.'

'No, it won't, not these days. They would have searched Mason's house, seen all the pictures, our marriage certificate. They would have asked around.'

Flynn rubbed the back of his neck. 'Leave them to it then. Let's sit tight, wait until they do.'

'No, Ned, I need to go back.'

Flynn's face reddened. 'Now that is a stupid thing to do.'

'No, what's stupid is waiting here, ignoring it.'

Flynn sighed. 'If they come and talk to you, just tell them you didn't know.'

'And how do you expect them to believe that when it's been on the local news and in the papers?'

'Just say you never saw it.'

'Don't be stupid, Ned. You know more than anyone what the police are like.'

'Exactly, you go back there now, and you'll make their job easy. They'll twist everything; have you as their prime suspect.'

'It's better than them coming here, asking questions about me, everyone in the village telling them about *you*.'

'Stop panicking. No one's going to come here. Let's give it more time. Like I said, we need to lie low.'

'What about your mother? This all started with you trying to help her. I could take her some money, keep her going until you can put things right.'

Flynn shook his head, even though it sounded tempting.

'You could write her a note,' she said. 'Put both your minds at rest.'

'No Nia, we can't risk it.'

She walked over to him and kissed him on the mouth. 'I still need to go back, Ned, find out what's happening. Believe me, it'll be fine. I'll be at my wit's end otherwise. I trusted you with the money, didn't I? So now you need to trust me.'

9

Nia only left three days ago, but to Flynn it seemed like weeks. He tried keeping himself busy, finding odd jobs to do; he even tried tidying the house. Whenever the doubt crept in, he worked faster, chiding himself, arguing that it was nothing but his imagination. Nia wouldn't let him down. She had too much to lose.

When he grew bored with the house, he strayed outside, deciding to chop some logs. He toiled like a man possessed, building up a sweat, the sun beating down on him. As he stacked the last of the logs, he peered through the shed window, noticing a black donkey jacket hanging from a nail, and wondered why he hadn't seen it before. He looked away, but the harder he tried not to think about it, the more it took shape in his mind. The idea took root, fleshed itself out, until all he could think about was the stranger, glaring at him in the woods. This time, he tried not to alarm himself. Haines was dead. There must be a rational explanation.

The man he'd encountered in the woods, that first night, could have been anybody, someone up to no good, a tramp, an addict, or a local miscreant. It had been a gloomy night, and he'd been walking for some time. But there was also another explanation. Perhaps it was Haines's ghost, keeping a close watch over Nia, warning him to keep his distance. A sudden feeling of unease crept over him. Flynn shook his head and smiled. He was Ned Flynn, for Christ's sake. He wasn't afraid. Men feared him.

Without a moment's pause, he left the garden and headed for the beach, his pace quickening, resolved to tame his imagination. Except for a couple walking their dog, the beach lay deserted. The tide was out, and seabirds scavenged along the shore. Flynn kept close to the water's edge, pressing hard into the polished sand. He'd half a mind to sprint across it, just as he had done when he was a kid. Such thoughts lightened his mood. He slowed his pace, then smiled, the absurdity of it all weakening his resolve. A stiff wind was rising, and grey clouds loomed in the distance. Flynn cut the walk short. One length of the shore was enough. He turned around and headed towards the woods; the threat of Haines's ghost fading as the urge to check on the money took root.

10

The markers he'd left brought him to the exact spot. Flynn took in the scene, satisfied to find the ground untouched. He considered digging it up, hiding it closer to home. The thought held him silent for a moment, but before he could act, he spotted someone near the slope, loitering among the trees. His gut reaction was to run towards it, face it head on. The slope was further away than he thought, steeper too, and took all his effort to climb it.

When Flynn reached the top, Bevan looked equally surprised and looked just as anxious. 'Jesus, Flynn, you scared the living daylights out of me. I wondered who the hell it was, chasing through the trees like a mad man.'

Flynn glanced at the bow saw in Bevan's hand. 'Why? Who did you think I was, someone catching you up to no good?'

Bevan smiled. 'I thought you might have been the forestry commission or something.'

'How long have you been here?'

Bevan shrugged. 'Not long, five or ten minutes at the most.'

'It's a bit out of your way, isn't it? I'm surprised you'd come here. There're trees all around your place.'

'Elder trees mostly, Hugh Cresswell asked me if I could get him some oak.'

Flynn stared at him for a moment, then glanced over at the trees, tracing the path he'd just followed. The spot where he'd buried the money wasn't visible from where he stood. Wild brambles and ivy-clad trees obscured the view, so he was certain Bevan hadn't seen a thing. He scoured the woods one last time, and when he turned around, Bevan was resting the saw on his shoulder.

'Are you going to use that?' Flynn said. 'I thought you were here for wood.'

Bevan glanced up at the tree next to him. 'They're all a bit too big here. I probably need to look further down or come back later with a chainsaw.'

Flynn rubbed his palm across his mouth. 'If you say so.' He looked towards a remote stretch of trees. 'Did you drive here?'

Bevan nodded.

'I suppose you won't mind giving me a lift?'

'I take it you're going home? What the hell were you doing out here, anyway?'

'Just fancied a walk; if that's okay with you?'

Bevan held out his palms. 'It's nothing to do with me; I was only asking.'

Flynn didn't answer, and they walked back to the Land Rover in silence.

11

Bevan had been driving a good fifteen minutes before Flynn spoke. 'What are you making him?'

Bevan kept his eyes on the road. 'What are you talking about?'

'Hugh Cresswell; we only spoke about it twenty minutes ago.'

Bevan veered towards the side of the road, slowing down as he clipped the hedge. 'Oh that, he wants... a coffee table or something. I can't remember.'

Flynn stared at him. 'Can't remember, hey?'

Bevan smiled. 'Yeah, I must be getting old.'

'Must be, but we can easily remedy that.'

'What d'you mean?'

'Let's drive to his house and ask him.'

Bevan pressed hard on the brakes and pulled up at the side of the road. 'Why do you want to do that, Flynn? Don't you believe me?'

'No, I don't. If you want to be a competent liar, then you need to have a great memory.'

Bevan's eyes widened. 'I'm not lying, Flynn. I'm telling you the truth. Why else would I be in those woods?'

Flynn shrugged. 'Spying on me.'

'Spying? Don't be so paranoid. Why would I do that?'

Flynn gripped Bevan's arm. 'I've no idea, you tell me.'

Bevan tried to pull away, but Flynn gripped his arm tighter. Bevan took a deep breath. 'I don't know what's going on in that head of yours, Flynn, but you're scaring me.'

Flynn released his arm. 'Good. You'd be wise to fear me.'

Bevan picked up his tobacco tin, flipped open the lid, and took out a thinly rolled cigarette. He popped it into his mouth, his hand trembling slightly as he flipped open his lighter. He took a deep drag and blew the smoke out of the window. 'I'm not lying to you, Flynn.'

'Fine,' Flynn said, 'but just for peace of mind, let's go see Hugh Cresswell.'

'Why? What's all this about?'

Flynn shook his head and grinned. 'I'll tell you later after we've seen Hugh Cresswell.'

Bevan took a drag of his cigarette, closing his eyes as he blew the smoke out. He shook his head and smiled 'There's a problem with that.'

'Go on.'

'Hugh Cresswell died three years ago.'

Flynn fixed his eyes on the road. 'Now we're getting somewhere. You better start talking.'

Bevan took another drag of his cigarette, this one deeper than the last. 'I was making sure you were all right. Nia came to see me. She's worried sick.'

'She seems to confide in you a lot these days; are you sleeping with her?'

'Don't talk like that, Flynn. I'm old enough to be her father.'

'Just about, what are you, fifty? That's not old, not for her anyway. Her husband was in his late sixties.' He stared Bevan in the eye. 'Did she tell you about him?'

Bevan nodded and threw his cigarette out of the window. 'She said he'd died.'

'That's it?'

'Said she was going home to sort a few things out.'

'And why did she ask you to watch me?'

Bevan sighed. 'She worries, all this time on your own, afraid you might start drinking. I'm concerned about you too. You've been acting peculiar, talking about seeing Haines's ghost.'

Flynn didn't answer, knowing Nia had every right to be worried. He was acting like an idiot. What was he thinking? The man had shown him nothing but good will.

12

Nia got home a little sooner than expected. Flynn had planned to meet her at the station, but she took an earlier train, then a taxi home. Flynn was all over her the minute she walked through the door. She looked taken aback at first. 'I've missed you too, Ned, but give me a chance to get into the house.'

He nodded and stepped aside, slightly hurt by her response, but masked it well. He helped her off with her coat, catching a whiff of her perfume. It was as though someone had just placed a bouquet in the house, a welcomed change from the reek of old cigarettes.

Nia kicked off her shoes and sank back onto the sofa. 'I'm exhausted. I could murder a cup of tea.'

'You relax,' he said. 'I'll make you one, and then you can tell me all about it.'

At first, she drank her tea in silence, savouring every sip. Then she locked her eyes on him, holding her cup in both hands. 'I needed that. There was nothing on the train.'

He nodded, trying his best to remain patient. He scanned her shape. God, she looked great in that dress.

She shot him a smile, as though she knew what he was thinking.

Flynn got up from his chair and sat next to her. 'So, how did it go?'

Nia shrugged. 'You know how it is.'

'Not really, I've little experience of widows going back to the scene of their husband's murder.'

She glared at him, his joke clearly unappreciated. 'It was like I said. I told the police who I was, then went to see Mason's solicitor.'

'And that was it?'

'Yeah, in a nutshell.'

'And the police never asked you anything?'

'They asked me things. They asked about Mason and me. How long have we been separated? Then they asked me to make a statement.'

'And that was it?'

'Yeah, kind of.'

'What do you mean, kind of?'

'They asked for my address, said they'd be in touch once they'd made progress.'

'I knew it.'

'What?'

'They're going to keep on at you. They won't leave you alone now.'

Nia sighed. 'I'm here, aren't I? Who's the one panicking now? I've already made a statement.'

Flynn couldn't believe what he was hearing. Things were becoming worse. What a foolish thing to do. He kept silent though, seeing as he created this mess in the first place. He should have given it more thought. But Mason would never have agreed. Men like him couldn't bear to lose. Flynn knew that, and Nia's body pressing against him reminded him it was all worth it.

'Stop winding yourself up,' she said. 'We're almost home and dry.'

He eased his hand down her back and kissed her neck. 'Almost?'

'There's the will. I'm waiting to hear from his solicitors.'

'I thought they would have already read that?'

'No, Ned, it needs to go probate.'

He shrugged. 'Whatever that means, how long's it going to take?'

Nia stood and walked to the other side of the room. She leaned against the windowsill, gazing into the garden. 'It'll be awhile, three to four weeks at least.'

The notion nettled him. He didn't like the sound of that. 'I don't know if I can wait that long? There's my mother to think about. She's been on her own for weeks now.'

She turned around. 'What happened to us sitting it out?'

'That was before.'

'Before what?'

'Before you made a statement.'

She chewed her bottom lip, then turned to face the window. 'Don't deny me this, Ned.'

'Deny you what, for Christ's sake?'

'My chance to get something back, that house is worth at least three-hundred thousand. It'll probably be mine in a few weeks.'

'Let me sleep on it,' he said, but looking at her, the yearning in her eyes, the wash of sunlight across her hair, he knew he could never deny her a thing.

PART III

THE WHISTLING SANDS

1

They did what Flynn said, lying low, minding their own business. Nia let the local authorities arrange the funeral which was Flynn's idea. 'Put your name to that,' he told her, 'and they'll hound you to pay the bill.'

She followed his advice. Well, up to a point. Even though Flynn insisted she shouldn't go, she still got Bevan to take her to the funeral.

'Someone might see you,' he said. He needn't have worried. There was barely anybody there: just the undertakers, hired bearers, a few mourners, and Nia dressed in a tight black dress, playing the grieving widow.

She acted strangely for a while when she got back home. She was cold and wistful, becoming tearful for no reason. Thankfully, it didn't last long. She soon snapped out of it, as though sensing Flynn was losing patience. Not that he gave her any signs. He was holding it together, and whenever the dead haunted him, he pushed such thoughts to the back of his mind.

Flynn kept fretting about his mother. He called her every other night.

'*Is that you, Ned?*' she'd say. '*Come home, I want to see you, son. I don't care what trouble you're in.*'

Flynn never said a word, his eyes glistening as he listened to the tenderness of her voice. He'd make it up to her soon; he'd see her right when this was over.

That morning started like any other. Nia got up early. Flynn had stayed in bed, stretching over to her side, lolling in her warmth. She hadn't disturbed him but had been a little louder than usual. He heard her murmuring, but didn't pay it much heed, figured it was one of her prayers. Then the front door slammed, the windows rattling in its wake.

Flynn just lay there, at first, a little startled, wondering what was going on. He closed his eyes and tried not to think about it, hoping he'd fall back to sleep. It was no use. Curiosity had taken hold, dragging him out of bed. He dressed and made his way downstairs. Nia had left the hall light on, and when he walked into the kitchen, there was an unfinished cup of coffee on the table. A torn envelope lay next to it, one of those official-looking types, brown and windowed. He picked it up and tried to read the postmark. All he could make out were the last two letters. He tossed it in the bin, scanned the room for the letter, but couldn't find it. Why care? If it were that important, Nia would show it to him when she got back. He gazed through the window, the roar in his stomach reminding him it was time for breakfast.

2

Flynn played with the food on his plate, every passing second making him more anxious. Where was she? She hadn't been this late for ages. He scraped back his chair and stood. 'To hell with it,' he said and put on his coat.

Flynn made his way to the sands, following the coastal path. Grey clouds drifted across the sky and the morning sun shied behind them. The air grew colder; the sea's tangy smell drifted in on the breeze. The path narrowed, and he followed it until it tapered off onto the beach. He stopped for a moment, watching the seabirds hovering above the water; their mewling cries growing fainter as each furious wave swept across the pebbled sands.

When he looked to his left, in the distance, where the sky met the land, he saw her. Nia's shape was unmistakable. She stood with her back to him, staring at another figure, a man, standing a few feet away.

The distance between them and the greying light obscured the man's face. In fact, the only features Flynn could make out was that the man was tall and broad-shouldered. Flynn started jogging towards them, making the stranger to turn and walk away.

Flynn was halfway across the sands before Nia noticed him. She looked startled, as though recently dragged from a dream. He called out to her, but she didn't answer. She just looked at him, a furious look on her face, as though Flynn's presence was an intrusion.

'Are you all right?' he said when he eventually reached her.

She grimaced. 'No, I'm not.'

'What's wrong? Was that guy bothering you?'

She threw him a bewildered look, then handed him a letter. 'It's from the solicitors. It came first thing this morning.'

Flynn held it close to his face, grazing over the words. He slid his hands to his sides. 'He never left you a thing.'

'No.' Her voice thickened. 'I didn't even know he had a sister.'

He wanted to console her but wasn't certain what to say. Instead, he stared past her, watching the figure fading as it reached the farthest reaches of the beach. 'Who is that?'

Nia turned her head, her eyes following Flynn's gaze. 'There's no one there, Flynn. Who are you talking about?'

'That man.' He pointed at the rocks. 'Look, over there, he's almost out of view.'

Nia cupped her hands around her eyes and turned her gaze to where Flynn was pointing. She kept it there for a minute before looking away. 'Sorry, I can't see anyone.'

Flynn shook his head and sighed. 'But you must have noticed him before? He was hardly a few feet away.'

'When?'

'Just now, he was standing in front of you on the beach.'

'I saw no one, Ned. You're the only person I've seen this morning.'

'But I saw him.'

'You saw something perhaps.'

'No, I saw a figure... a man.'

She didn't say a word, just stared at him.

'You think I'm crazy, don't you?'

She shook her head. 'No, I don't. It's–'

'What?'

'We've both been under a lot of pressure lately with all this stuff about Mason.'

Flynn didn't answer, both of them staying quiet as they made their way back. Nia took the lead, trudging ahead, with Flynn trailing behind her. The wind grew fiercer with every sudden gust. Flynn's mind wandered. His thoughts caught between the man he'd seen on the sands, and Nia's perfect figure in front of him. He wanted her more than ever now. He hated the power Haines had over them, swearing to keep her close, vowing that no man, alive or dead, would ever come between them.

3

Nia wouldn't stop talking about it. This surprised Flynn. He'd never known her to be so insistent. 'I keep telling you why,' he said. 'We need to lie low.'

She took a deep breath. 'But we already have, for weeks.'

He stared at her. The look on his face couldn't have been more incredulous. 'That suited you fine while you were waiting to hear about the will.'

'Things have changed now. I was hoping to get more for us. But even in death, Mason likes to win.'

She gave Flynn that sad look. The one that frequently caused him give in. 'It's time to move on, Flynn, before any more trouble gets delivered to our door.'

The voice inside his head told him she was right. 'I need to take care of my mother first until I do that we're going nowhere.'

Nia sighed. 'So why don't you do that? You call her every other night. Why don't you speak to her, for God's sake?'

A hint of accusation laced her voice. The way she said it made him sound crazy. A pained look fixed in her eyes. The same look he'd seen yesterday, when he'd asked who the man was on the beach.

'I'm going to sort it out soon,' he said. 'It's not just the money. I need to find someone to take care of her.'

'So why don't we do it now?'

'You what?'

'Why don't we sort things out for your mother now? Then we can leave.'

'I will, just give me a few more weeks.'

He knew how pathetic it sounded, a man searching for an excuse. But he needed more time. He couldn't explain why. He just felt it. The prospect of going back there now made him uneasy. He was tired of seeing the dead. One ghost was bad enough.

'We need to be careful,' he said, trying to explain himself.

'Perhaps we're being too careful,' Nia said through a sigh. 'I've been back twice now, and nothing's happened. No one's connecting you with Mason. Why don't you take a chance?'

'Because that's what I've always done. No, we'll stay here until the time's right. I've spent half my life in prison owing to people asking me *to take a chance*.'

4

They eventually found a compromise. They'd wait a little longer, and Flynn agreed that he'd arrange things for his mother in a few weeks. Nia seemed satisfied by that. 'It's a start I suppose, but the sooner we leave, the better. This place isn't good for you.'

He knew what she meant, but he didn't dare to say a word. She was trying her best, and although it pained him to see her make so many sacrifices, he was happy not to hear her prayers and loved seeing her next to him every morning in bed.

Flynn was trying too, mostly by keeping things to himself. He never mentioned the potent smell of pipe tobacco lingering in the hall and ignored the strange happenings in the house: ornaments smashed on the floor, a kitchen chair lying on its side. Some nights he woke to the sound of knocking on the front door. When he looked outside, he'd see no one, just the glimpse of a man's shadow.

The nights were the worst, in the hours after they'd made love when Nia had fallen asleep. The strangest notions plagued his mind. When he'd first told Nia about his father's illness, Flynn didn't pay it much heed. He knew he had his old man's temper. Why shouldn't he? It was a natural process; a curse passed down from father to son. To hear Flynn, talk about it, you'd think he was a psychiatrist. He could speak as much psychobabble as the best of them. The counselling sessions in prison had enabled him to tap into the sources of his anger. Not that it helped that much. Instead of rejecting his violent urges, he embraced them, justified them, concluding that every bad thing he'd ever done was because of the suffering caused to him in the past. Seeing ghosts was entirely different. It was the strangest feeling. A vision associated with liars, the lonely, and the deluded. He wondered which one he was, concluding he was probably all three.

5

When Flynn asked Nia about the mess in the lounge, she told him she'd no idea.

'One of us probably left a window open,' she said, 'or slammed the door or something.'

Flynn remained unconvinced. 'It must have been one hell of a slam to turn over a small table and hurl it to the middle of the room. The weather's been mild. I don't remember any nine-force gales.'

Nia picked up the plant table and put it back in the corner. Then she fetched a dustpan and brush and started cleaning up the mess. She carried the Peace Lily by its roots, glanced at Flynn and said, 'We need to replant it.'

He murmured something, then went outside to the shed. As Flynn glanced through the shed window, the knot in his stomach tightened. Someone had trashed the place; tools were thrown about; nails and screws were tipped onto the workbench; and splatters of red paint marked the floor. Someone must have broken in, without smashing the windows, or busting the lock. He looked at it for a second, then went back into the house. 'Nia, have you seen the state of the shed?'

She stayed by the sink, clipping the dead leaves from the plant. She kept her eyes fixed on it. 'No, why? What about it?'

'Come outside, you need to look at this.'

She set the plant down on the draining board, sighed, and accompanied him into the garden. As she neared the shed, Flynn unlocked the door. A putrid smell tainted the air, forcing them both to step back. Flynn covered his nose. 'Jesus, I can taste that. It's like someone died in here.'

Nia took a closer look. 'Except for the smell, what's the problem?'

'Look at the state of the place.'

'Perhaps it's been like this for a while.'

'It was fine the other morning.'

She walked further inside and glanced around, placing her hand over her mouth as she fixed on something in the corner. Flynn followed her gaze and saw she was staring at a watch. He brushed past her and bent down to pick it up.

'Leave it,' she said.

He stood and turned around, about to ask why she'd yelled at him, but the frightened look on her face changed his mind. 'What's wrong?'

She nodded at the watch. 'That was Martin's. I thought he was wearing it the day he–'

Flynn took her arm and led her outside. He tried to keep it together, for her sake, although he was equally shaken. He ushered her into the house and made her sit down on the sofa. She said nothing, staring straight ahead.

Flynn didn't like to see her like this, but he felt relieved. She saw stuff too, so at least he wasn't going crazy. He glanced towards the kitchen. 'Do you want a cup of tea or something?'

'I'm fine.'

He sat beside her and lay his hand on her lap. 'There's some weird shit happening today.' He'd tried to make a joke of it, but the note of laughter in his voice only made him sound nervous.

Nia turned to face him. 'I thought Martin wore that watch the day he drowned.' She took a deep breath. 'I must have been mistaken.'

Flynn nodded. 'I guess so. It's strange, though, don't you think, the house, the watch turning up out of nowhere, and all that mess in the shed?'

Nia held herself. 'I don't know. It was probably there all the time. That stuff just toppled over or something. There's bound to be an explanation.'

Flynn moved his hand away. 'There's an explanation all right.'

Nia stood up. 'Don't start, Ned.'

'What?'

'I know where this is heading. Bevan told me.'

'Told you what?'

'About the troubles you've been having?'

'Troubles?'

'You know what I'm speaking about. The things you've supposed to have seen in the woods, and out on the sands.'

Flynn couldn't believe what he was hearing. All this time, all he'd done was try to stop her from worrying by keeping things to himself. But here she was, going behind his back at any opportunity. 'What prompted him to tell you that?'

'I spoke to him the other morning when I got the letter about the will.'

'You spoke to *him*?'

'I was upset, Ned. I needed to talk to someone.'

He forced a laugh. 'Did you not think about talking to me?'

'You were asleep. Anyway, I knew what you'd say. I wanted to get another opinion.'

'An opinion on what?'

'The will, I wasn't sure what to do.'

Flynn stood and clutched her arms. She looked frightened. Serves her right, he thought. If she was happy to go behind his back and confide in Bevan, then he'd give her something to be afraid of. 'Jesus, Nia, what the hell have you told him?'

She pulled away from him. 'Nothing, we talked about the will.'

'And you've never told him about Mason?'

'What do you take me for? I can't believe you'd ask me that. No, I'd never tell him a thing.'

'You asked him to spy on me, though.'

'I asked him to keep an eye on you. For Christ's sake, Ned, stop being so paranoid. I was worried about you.'

'And that's why he told you about *my problems,* I suppose?'

She didn't say a thing. She didn't have to. He already knew the answer.

He stared at her for a few seconds. 'Bevan told you about what I'd seen?'

She nodded.

'You've seen him too?'

She shook her head. 'No, only in my dreams.'

He didn't like her answer; it implied an intimacy that only he and Nia should be a part of. And why should she be able to dream while he was stuck in this nightmare? 'What do you make of all this?'

'I don't know.'

'What d'you mean, you don't know? You're supposed to believe in all this stuff.'

'I believe in the afterlife, yes, but I'm a Methodist, not a Spiritualist. That's a different faith.'

'Are these signs of the afterlife then, or is it just me going crazy?'

Her eyes glistened. 'I don't know what it is. All I know is, this place isn't good for you.'

6

After they'd made love, they lay naked together in bed. Flynn hadn't felt this close to her for weeks, not since he'd returned from Mason's. The night's silence soothed him, as did the gentle murmur of her breath. Nia's body felt warm. She lay her head on his chest, the gentle glow of the lights falling across her shoulders. He wanted to hold on to this moment forever because, like every good thing in his life, he knew it wouldn't last. In an hour, it would be just another memory. As much as he tried to savour it, he couldn't stop feeling guilty. He needed to get back home, start sorting things out for his mother. Perhaps Nia was right. Maybe they'd been here too long. Part of him wanted to tell her this, but he kept silent, following his gut, realising it was still too soon to chance it.

He needed to say something, compliment her, and tell her how he felt. But he didn't know what to say. Words had never been his thing. Instead, he eased his hand across her back and whispered, 'Thanks.'

Without lifting her head, Nia said, 'For what?'

'Worrying, keeping an eye on me.'

She kissed his chest, stroked a finger down his stomach, following its thin trail of hair. His skin prickled, and he closed his eyes as her hand rested beneath the sheet.

'You sounded different,' she said.

'When?'

'Just now.'

'In what way?'

'There was something in your voice, a gentleness, as if you'd realised I've been trying to help you. You know this is the first time I've felt your trust.'

Flynn opened his eyes. 'Yes, I trust you. What makes you think I don't?'

She sighed, pushed herself up, and leaned back into her pillow. 'The things you say. The way you look at me sometimes.'

'What do you mean the way I look at you?'

'As if I'm always up to something. You remind me of those bastards in the village, looking at me as if I'm the worst kind of poison.'

Flynn sat up. 'I'm nothing like them.'

'I know nothing about you. And you've told me nothing about what happened between you and Mason.'

She always called the old man Mason now. When she and Flynn had first met, she'd referred to Mason as her ex, as though refusing to say his name. It was her way of detaching herself, he guessed, allowing her to add more distance. Flynn told her everything about that night. How Mason had lost his temper and the vile things he'd said.

Nia seemed troubled by that. 'Did you believe him?'

Flynn shook his head, and trying to sound nonchalant said, 'No.'

She stared at him. 'I'm not like that, you know.'

He reached across the bedside table and grabbed his pack of cigarettes. 'I never said you were.'

He lit a cigarette, only taking one drag before Nia snatched it from his mouth. She held it between her fingers, as though she'd been smoking for years. 'It's all lies. Mason, like most men, gets ugly when he can't have his own way.'

She handed him the cigarette. 'I'm not that person, Ned.'

'What person?'

'The conniving whore that everybody says I am.'

'When have I ever said that?'

She turned her back on him, slapping her head down on the pillow. 'You don't need to.'

'What's that supposed to mean?'

'You question everything I do. I daren't go anywhere.'

'We keep going over this. I'm just trying to be careful. Jesus, Nia, I thought I was the one who was paranoid.'

He put his hands on her shoulders and turned her towards him. He could have looked at her all night, held silent by the radiance of her skin. But it was her eyes that beguiled him the most; he felt powerless staring into them. 'Of course, I trust you. What can I do to prove it?'

She nestled into him, and he could smell a trace of lavender in her hair. She clutched his hand, pushing her fingers through his. 'You could give me the money. I could set things up for us, buy a small bar, Spain or something.'

Flynn forced a laugh. 'And what will I do.'

'Sort things out for your mother, and then you can join me in two weeks.'

'I dunno... Spain, and what do you know about running bars?'

'Quite a lot. I used to manage a few. Before I met Martin, Mason was going to buy me one.'

Flynn breathed deeply, rubbed the whiskers on his chin.

'I need you with me, especially with what's been going on. There's no way I can deal with it on my own.'

She clutched his hand tighter. 'Sure, whatever you say, but at least let me make myself useful.'

'You're doing enough as it is.'

She let go of his hand and sat up. 'No, I'm not. If we're going to stay here for a while, then I may as well call Mason's solicitor.'

He gave her a baffled look.

'It was Bevan's idea; said I'd be a fool not to contest the will.'

7

Flynn brooded over it for hours. In fact, it kept him awake most of the night. How dare Bevan say that, making things worse, sticking his nose into people's business. It surprised him that Bevan mentioned it. He credited him with more sense. Bevan thought he was doing the right thing. Why wouldn't he? He'd no idea about Mason. No matter how good the intention, Flynn was sick of him interfering.

That morning, as Flynn walked to Bevan's house, he rehearsed the scene in his mind. He already knew what he was going to say. But to keep Nia quiet, he needed to keep it friendly. He hadn't walked this route for a while and was struck by the changes in the trees. The autumn colours were fading, making way for a colder season. Not that it bothered him. He'd be long gone before the frost set in, spending his Christmas on some faraway Spanish beach. The thought cheered him, and he quickened his pace.

Twenty minutes later, he was hammering on Bevan's door. When no one answered, he went around the back.

Bevan's Land Rover stood in its usual spot, but there was another car there too. Flynn hadn't seen it before, a white VW Passat, one of the earlier models.

As Flynn peeped through the kitchen window, Bevan opened the door. Bevan looked rough. His piggy eyes almost shut, his skin blotchy and puffed.

'I've been knocking for a while,' Flynn said.

Bevan yawned and rubbed his eyes. 'Sorry, I must have dropped off.'

'Must have,' Flynn said and followed him into the house.

The lounge smelled awful, as though somebody had just died there. Bevan must have read Flynn's expression because he quickly opened the window. He gestured for Flynn to sit down, and Flynn chose the chair in the corner. He sat facing the kitchen, staring at the crate of empty beer bottles near the fridge. He glanced at Bevan and smiled. 'Looks like you've been celebrating.'

Bevan nodded and sat down, slowly, as though it was a strain for him. 'I had a little family reunion. Ronnie came to see me, my nephew. He's going to stay here for a while.'

As if on cue, someone stomped across the landing, yawned, let out a huge belch, and then hurried downstairs.

Ronnie, wearing only a faded pair of jeans, thrust open the door. He nodded at Bevan and then slumped down next to him on the sofa. He glared at Flynn for a second, giving him a look that said, 'Who the hell are you?'

Ronnie pushed his long, blond hair back and tied it into a ponytail. He was about six-four. His shoulders were enormous, and his tattooed arms almost wider than Bevan's thighs. The cocksure look in Ronnie's eyes reminded Flynn of his younger self. He couldn't decide whether Ronnie had yet to meet his match, or he'd earned the look through experience. He'd seen his type before. There were loads of men like Ronnie, almost one in every bar. Most of them were full of crap, building a reputation for themselves by choosing their fights carefully. Then they'd live off the myth, keeping most men frightened or befriending those who weren't. But there was something different about Ronnie. Something in his eyes that hinted he was for real.

Bevan glanced at his nephew. 'Ronnie, this is Flynn.'

Ronnie nodded. 'I figured that out for myself.' He scanned Flynn's shape; an unimpressed look settled on his face. 'So, you're the notorious Ned Flynn, hey. I've heard a lot about you.' Most men would have offered their hand, but Ronnie just sat there.

Flynn stared at him for a second. 'So what have you heard, good things I hope?'

Ronnie grinned. 'Depends what you mean by good.' He placed his hands behind his head. 'I've heard you're a dangerous man.' There was a hint of disdain in his voice. 'A *Professional Boxer.*'

Flynn smiled to himself. 'That was a long time ago.'

'What have you been doing since?'

'This and that.'

'*This* and *that*?'

'If you must know, I spent a bit of time inside.'

'Wandsworth?'

Flynn shook his head. 'Walton and what's with all the questions.'

Ronnie sat up. 'I'm just showing an interest, that's all, being friendly to my uncle's guest.'

Flynn fixed him with a stare. 'You've got a strange way of being friendly.'

As Ronnie was about to say something, Bevan leaned

forward and clapped his hands. 'So, Flynn, what brings you up here this morning?'

Flynn looked at Bevan. 'I need to talk to you about something.'

Bevan leaned back into the sofa, nodded, then said, 'Okay.'

Flynn glanced at Ronnie. 'It's a little sensitive.'

Bevan smiled. 'Don't worry about him. He's family. Just say what you need to say.'

Flynn sighed. 'Okay, if that's how you prefer it.' He rested his hands on his lap. 'It's about Nia. She said you and her had a brief chat.'

'That's right,' Bevan said. 'She was upset about a few things. I gave her some advice.'

Flynn sighed. 'That's what I'm here to talk about. I'd prefer it if you'd keep your advice to yourself.'

'That's selfish,' Ronnie said, becoming silent as Bevan held out his palm.

Bevan stood up. 'Come on, Flynn, let's get a coffee.'

Flynn followed him into the kitchen. He stood by the fridge, facing the window. Bevan flicked on the kettle, then went over to the sink and rinsed out two cups. The task took longer than it should have, Bevan's hands shaking throughout. He placed the cups on the draining board. Then he gripped the edge of the sink, resting his weight on it, breathing deeply.

'You all right?' Flynn said.

Bevan nodded. 'Just give me a minute. I've never been one for drinking.'

'You should go back to bed.'

Bevan cast him a glance. 'I thought you didn't like people giving advice.'

Flynn laughed. 'I'd just prefer it if you'd ease off. We've

enough going on as it is. I don't want anyone filling Nia's head with stupid notions.'

Bevan shuffled over to the kettle. 'And what notions might they be?'

Flynn listened to the water boiling and watched a billow of steam rising to the ceiling. He kept quiet as Bevan put the coffee into the cups, then said, 'All this stuff about contesting the will.'

Bevan picked up the kettle and poured the boiling water into the cups, the smell of hot coffee rising. 'I didn't mean any harm. I just think she's entitled to something.' He added the milk and sugar, then handed Flynn a cup. 'Especially after everything she's been through.'

Flynn took a sip of coffee, its cheap bitterness sticking to the roof of his mouth. 'I know that, but next time, keep Nia out of it. If you've got any bright ideas come and talk to me.'

Ronnie stood in the doorway with his big arms folded across his chest. 'And who the hell are you to give my uncle orders?'

Six months ago, Flynn wouldn't have hesitated. He'd have leapt onto Ronnie in a flash, punching and kicking until one of them was left for dead. But things had changed since then. And as much as he wanted to rip Ronnie's heart out, he needed to keep a low profile.

Instead, Flynn just glanced at him, smiled, then ambled to the back door. He put one foot outside, paused, and looked over his shoulder. 'Thinking about it, Bevan, there's no need to come to me. In fact, I think we'd all be better off if you and that retarded nephew of yours kept such notions to yourselves.'

Ronnie motioned towards him, growing more frustrated as Bevan stood in his way.

'You want to watch your mouth,' Ronnie said, becoming quiet as Bevan whispered something into his ear.

Flynn turned his back on them and stepped into the garden. He felt pleased with himself. Perhaps he was getting wiser after all. He'd always met trouble head-on. These days, he was managing to walk away.

8

Flynn had only been up for half an hour when the white Passat pulled outside the house. Thankfully, Nia was out shopping. She'd be gone for a while. She hated going to the village, so Bevan had driven her into town.

Flynn stood by the window, watching Ronnie get out of the car. Ronnie slammed the car door, shoved open the gate, and swaggered up the path. He had something under his arm, a bottle of some sort. Flynn didn't answer at first. He let Ronnie wait for a while, grinning to himself, as the knocking grew more ferocious. Then, just as Ronnie turned to leave, Flynn opened the bedroom window. 'What do you want?'

'I've come to apologise,' Ronnie said. He held out a bottle of whisky. 'I've brought a peace offering.'

'I'm off the drink for a while. Another time perhaps.'

'Come on,' Ronnie pleaded. 'I'm trying my best here. At least invite me in.'

Flynn sighed. 'I suppose. Come around the back.'

Ronnie wasn't shy. As soon as Flynn let him in, he strode

into the lounge and sat down on the sofa. 'Nice place, your wife's called Nia, right?'

Flynn stood by the door. 'Yeah, but she's not my wife.'

'But you live together, so technically it's the same thing.'

Flynn nodded, pretending to give it some thought. After a brief silence, Ronnie grinned and gave the bottle a shake. 'Why don't you fetch some glasses and join me in a drink.'

Flynn glanced up at the clock. 'It's not even ten.'

'So?'

'So, *technically*, that's too early.'

Ronnie shook the bottle again. 'Come on, you don't strike me as a man who's a stickler for convention. Guys like us make our own rules. Let's have a drink; let me apologise for Christ's sake.'

Flynn went into the kitchen, and a minute later stepped back into the lounge holding two small glasses. He held them in front of him as Ronnie poured the whisky. Ronnie took a glass and raised it to his lips, pausing before he took a sip. 'Iechyd da.'

Flynn gave him a bemused look.

'It's Welsh for *Good Health*,' Ronnie said, 'or so Bevan tells me.'

Flynn took a sip of whisky and sat in the chair opposite. He studied Ronnie for a second, trying not to smile at the way he was dressed. He wore a black t-shirt, faded jeans and a jacket to match. His black leather cowboy boots had a Chinese dragon embossed on both ankles. All he was lacking was the hat.

'Nice boots,' Flynn said.

Ronnie beamed. 'I think so too. Found them on the internet, been searching for a pair like this for ages. Fancied something different.'

Flynn smiled. 'Well, they're unique, that's for sure.'

'Exactly. A man needs to look his best.'

'I guess,' Flynn said. 'I've never really been one for clothes.'

Ronnie grinned. 'No, I can see that.'

Flynn shook his head and sipped his whisky. 'And this is your way of apologising?'

Ronnie laughed. 'No, I'm just messing with you, that's all.'

'You're a real joker.'

'That's me. Life's too short to be serious.'

Flynn necked his whisky in one and held out his glass for a refill. 'You seemed serious yesterday.'

Ronnie poured more whisky into Flynn's glass. 'Yeah, that's what I came to talk about.'

'Go on,' Flynn said. 'I'm listening.'

Ronnie swirled the whisky in his glass. 'I'd been drinking all day and night. I felt like shit yesterday morning. You know how it is. You look for someone to take it out on.' He kept his eyes fixed on the carpet. 'I'm sorry, all right.'

A while back, Flynn would have made a bigger deal of it. He would have dragged it out more, probably made him beg for forgiveness. For Nia's sake, he just nodded. 'No problem, apology accepted.'

Flynn rested the glass on his lap. 'So how much of this was Bevan's idea?'

Ronnie shrugged. 'It was fifty-fifty.' He glanced up at Flynn. 'Can I be honest with you?'

'Sure.'

'I don't deny that most of what happened yesterday was because of me. But you didn't help things. I'm very fond of my uncle, and I'm not starting anything, but I don't like people telling him what to do.'

'That's understandable. Family's family.' Flynn necked

down the second glass of whisky, then slapped his free hand down onto his chest. He took a deep breath, his eyes watering. 'Me and Nia have been under a lot of pressure lately.'

'And you don't want anyone interfering?'

'It's not just that. It's a combination of things. We've had a run of bad luck. Things just got on top of me.'

Ronnie leaned forward and filled up Flynn's glass. 'Well, I'm here to remedy that.'

'How d'you mean?'

'Because as soon as we finish this bottle, we're going to the pub.'

9

At first, Flynn was hesitant to leave the house, but Ronnie remained relentless, finally persuading him. It was a smooth drive to the village, considering Ronnie had just drunk half a bottle of whisky. Once Ronnie started talking, it was difficult to shut him up. He kept jumping from one subject to another, jabbering on like a machine gun. It was a pleasant change, though, reminding Flynn of the old days. Flynn hadn't enjoyed the crack like this in ages. But he'd stop laughing now and then, grow pensive, especially when the guilt kicked in.

After parking the car, they went to the Old Bell. Not that they had any choice. There were only two pubs in the village, and Flynn was barred from one of them. He'd only been here once before, and as he stood by the bar, he knew why. It reminded him of those dingy, old pubs of his childhood, where his mother used to send him to fetch his dad. The place probably looked different in the summer months; the dark mahogany furniture washed in light, and the silence drowned out by laughter. But it was late autumn now, and the pub was cold and deserted.

'We'll go after we finish these,' Ronnie said, as though reading Flynn's mind. 'This place is like a graveyard.'

Flynn smiled. 'I'd get used to it if I were you. I'm barred from the White Lion. So, this graveyard's our only choice.'

Ronnie necked down his pint, slammed the glass down on the table. 'You're kidding me, right? We'll just go to the White Lion for Christ's sake. Who's going to say anything to us?'

Flynn's gut reaction was to agree. Then he changed his mind. Things were different now. He mulled it over for a few minutes, drawn to both sides of the coin, part of him wanting to prove something, save face, and show Ronnie what he was made of. Another part told him it wasn't worth it, demanded he kept a low profile. Then he thought to hell with it. What did he have to lose? All they could do was chuck him out.

When they arrived at the White Lion, a young barmaid served them. Flynn hadn't seen her before and assumed she must be new.

'I told ya,' Ronnie said, 'nothing to worry about.'

Flynn nodded, realising it was only a matter of time. The landlord was bound to spot him, eventually. In the meantime, he'd enjoy a drink. He may as well make the most of it. Flynn chose the table nearest the fire. The same place he had sat when he first arrived here. It seemed so long ago. And for a second, he wished he could go back in time and warn himself.

'What's wrong with you?' Ronnie said. 'You've gone all quiet on me.'

'Nothing, I was just thinking.'

Ronnie glanced around the room. 'This place needs some noise.' He stood up and wandered over to the internet jukebox. A few minutes later, the dulcet notes of Marty

Robbins' *El Paso* filled the room. On his way back to the table, Ronnie asked the barmaid to turn it up. She did so with no fuss, her smile a little too obliging. He threw her a wink which seemed to please her, then sat down and took a long swig of his pint. 'I don't know about you, Flynn. But it looks like I'm sorted.'

Flynn glanced at the bar. 'She seems to like cowboys.'

Ronnie laughed. 'It's my dad's fault, brainwashed me from an early age. He was obsessed with the Wild West, especially Country 'n Western.'

'Is that what brought you here?'

'How d'you mean?'

'The Wild West of Wales.'

Ronnie grinned. 'Not entirely, I thought it was time to see my uncle, haven't seen him for ages.'

'You've kept in touch though, hey?'

'Yeah, he's always texting me and shit. We've always been very close.'

'That surprises me, to be honest.'

Ronnie sat up in his chair, 'Why?'

'Bevan has never spoken of you.'

Ronnie picked up his glass and drained the last drop of beer into his mouth. He kept hold of it, clutching it tightly, as though trying to break it. 'You know what he's like. He keeps most things to himself.'

Flynn nodded, then glanced down at the table. 'He seems to share a lot with Nia, though.'

Ronnie opened his mouth to say something, pausing as Glenn Campbell's *Gentle on My Mind* held him silent. He closed his eyes for a second and sighed. 'Gets me every time this song, those words are poetry.'

'I guess,' Flynn said. 'I've always preferred something more upbeat. Sad songs depress me.'

Ronnie scraped back his chair and stood. 'The only depressing things here are those empty glasses on the table.' He held out his hand as Flynn motioned to get up. 'You stay where you are. The first few are on me.'

Flynn watched him as he strolled over to the bar. The barmaid who'd been chattering with an old couple at the far end, dashed over the moment she saw him. She looked in her early twenties, her skin glowing, a small rose tattooed on her neck. The young woman became more striking the longer Flynn watched her. She had a somewhat oriental look about her, white Chinese mix. The way she eyed Ronnie filled Flynn with resentment. Nia hadn't looked at him like that for ages. He glanced up at the clock. One more drink and he would make his way home. Make sure he was there when Nia got back.

'What's wrong with you now?' Ronnie said as he put the drinks down on the table.

Flynn didn't respond at first, but when Ronnie kept staring at him, he mumbled he was fine.

Ronnie sat down. 'Fine, hey? The look on your face says otherwise. I hope when I get to your age I don't look as miserable as that.'

Flynn picked up his pint and took a swig. 'I'm not that old. You keep talking to me like that, and you won't get to reach thirty.'

Ronnie laughed. 'That's more like it.'

Flynn necked down the rest of his pint, then banged the glass down on the table. 'Listen, I need to go.'

Ronnie shook his head and sighed, 'No way. Come on, Flynn. We've only just started.' He glanced over his shoulder at the barmaid, and, lowering his voice, said, 'Tanya's invited me for a coffee when she finishes work, so you need to keep me company till then.'

Flynn agreed to stay for a few more, although he needed little persuading. He tried to pace himself, but by late evening, he was drunk. He hid it well. The only thing that gave him away was that he kept talking. It was Ronnie's fault; he kept spurring him on, listening attentively while Flynn shared his stories. Ronnie told a few of his own, but they sounded trivial compared to Flynn's.

Flynn told him about his boxing and how he'd ended up inside. He spoke about his mother, the drink making him sentimental. He told Ronnie how much he loved her, and how much he loved Nia too.

'Is that why you're staying here?' Ronnie said. He threw the room a disapproving glance. 'Because I sure as hell can't think of any other reason.'

Flynn nodded, the voice in his head telling him he'd said too much. He took a deep breath, stood up and ambled towards the gents. The smell of the toilets almost made him puke, a recent mix of bleach and urine. He stood at the urinal, watching his aim as he took a piss. When he was finished, he staggered over to the sink, washed his hands, then rinsed his face with cold water. As he looked in the mirror, the face that looked back startled him. This wasn't how he pictured himself. He was pale, gaunt, and baggy-eyed. He was only in his mid-thirties, but he looked like a man on the cusp of old age. There was sorrow in his eyes. Something he hadn't noticed since he was a kid. Surely, this couldn't be him. The man in the mirror looked so tormented.

When Flynn got back, Ronnie was talking with Tanya, whispering into her ear, filling the room with her raucous laughter. Flynn staggered over to them and leaned against the bar. He looked up at the clock, surprised that it was almost ten-thirty. He placed a hand on Ronnie's shoulder, told him he was going home. This time, Ronnie didn't try to stop him. He just nodded, as though agreeing that Flynn had had enough.

Tanya shot Flynn a smile. 'Do you want me to call you a Taxi?'

'No need for that,' Ronnie said. He gave Flynn a wink. 'A taxi will get him home too soon. This man needs to sober up.' He smoothed his hand down Tanya's arm. 'I'll walk with him part of the way, shouldn't be that long. Don't you leave without me.'

She stroked his hand for a second; a hint of promise glistened in her brown eyes.

10

The night was a sombre scene of damp and mist. A dog yapped in the distance, and the amber street-lights cast ominous shadows. Flynn raised his collar, inhaling a cold blast of air. He staggered at first, but quickly took stock of himself. Ronnie was drunk too, but not as much as Flynn had hoped. He'd planned to out-drink him, put the youngster in his place. But it was Flynn who was worse for wear. They said little as they left the village, just the occasional complaint about the cold. Every so often Ronnie grabbed Flynn's arm and guided him back onto the path.

When they approached the crossroads, Ronnie stopped. He gazed into the dark, sighed, then lay a hand on Flynn's shoulder. 'Well, old man, this is where I have to leave you.' He pointed to an opening in the trees. 'That's your quickest way.'

Flynn searched his pocket for a cigarette. 'And how the hell would you know?'

'Uncle Bevan took me on a tour the other day, showed me all the shortcuts.'

Flynn lit a cigarette, then flicked it into the grass, the smell of the smoke almost making him retch. 'And why was Bevan showing you a shortcut to my house?'

'I didn't know it was your house until this morning.'

Flynn glanced into the woods. 'Nah, I'm going to keep to the road. Like you said before, I better try to sober up.'

'Suit yourself, it's a fair way though. You'll sober up, I suppose. Either that or you'll die from pneumonia.' Ronnie put his hands in his pockets and stepped back. 'I guess you're big and ugly enough to look after yourself.' He grinned. 'Anyway, I've got better things to do.'

Flynn stood there for a while, watching Ronnie make his way back. Every few seconds Ronnie turned around and pointed at the trees. Eventually, Flynn gave in. He was tired and cold, and as Ronnie shouted something, he thought to hell with it and edged his way into the woods.

11

The lofty trees provided more shelter than the open road, but beneath a gloomy sky it took Flynn a while to adapt to the darkness. Occasionally he swayed to one side, keeping his eyes focused on the path, trying his best not to slip. A sickly feeling settled in his stomach, forcing him to take deep breaths. Flynn's legs weakened with every step, and he felt certain they'd eventually give way.

As he made his way home, Flynn's mind wandered. It was always the case when he'd had a drink, his imagination presenting him with all kinds of scenarios. Not that he needed much encouragement these days, and he tried hard to keep the darker thoughts at bay. Instead, he thought about Nia, picturing her by his side as they lay down on a beach somewhere in the Costa del Sol. He'd bring his mother with them too. Flynn's mother had never been abroad. In fact, she'd never wandered further than a hundred miles from her home. A pang of sadness stabbed at his heart. His mother's life had been one struggle after the next, and he assured himself it was about to change.

Things were going to change for him and Nia too. They were soulmates, and except for his mother, she was the only person he could trust. Admittedly, he needed to give her more space, be less possessive. Nia wasn't a woman to be controlled. You couldn't collar her like some prized feline and parade her around on a leash. He'd learned that the hard way. Jealousy was no man's friend, and he had no intention of ending up like Mason.

Thinking of the old man made him aware of the dark, the night's silence, and the mist settling between the trees. The muted glow of the moon gave the woods less shadow, and except for the occasional clatter in the trees, the night stood silent.

As the path tapered off into the road, Flynn quickened his pace. He still felt unsteady on his feet, but found momentum in the thought of Nia waiting up for him. The cottage came into sight, snuggled among the trees against a backdrop of black hills. The light from the downstairs window spilt onto the grass, and a glow of pale yellow brushed across the top of the fence. As he drew nearer, Flynn glanced at the fields, pausing when he caught sight of something in the mist. It was difficult to make out what it was at first, and for a second, he thought it was nothing but a trick of the light. Then it moved, only slightly, but enough to distinguish its outline. The figure stood tall and broad, a hazed silhouette standing about fifteen feet away. Flynn clenched his fists, subduing the panic within. He'd always done that. Where most men would turn and run, he would stand his ground. He'd done it since he was a kid; his old man had made sure of it. Violence was the only way he knew. He wasn't afraid of a living soul, yet violence was no match for the dead.

'Hey' Flynn shouted, then coughed at the dryness in his

throat. He stared into the mist, waiting for something to move. 'Hey,' he said, again, but nothing stirred; the only sound was his heart thumping against the silence.

After a few minutes, Flynn turned around, an icy breeze settling across his back. The gate creaked open with a shove, and Flynn staggered down the garden path. He stopped when he reached the front door, and with his head bowed, rummaged through his pockets for his key. It took him a while to find it, and he felt a great sense of achievement as he clutched it in his hand. He held it between his finger and thumb and raised his head to the door.

Flynn dropped the key the moment he saw Haines's reflection. Its skin was moon-white, its grimaced mouth smeared with blood, and its dark eyes full of hate. Flynn cried out, a pathetic, child-like shriek. On trying to turn, his knees bent, and he buckled to the ground, swinging blows at the darkness. 'Haines,' he cried, falling silent when a sharp wedge of light settled over him, and two soft, warm hands tried to pull him up. He let them guide him to his knees, then raised his head, the shock subsiding.

Nia shot him an alarmed look. 'What's happened, Ned? I heard you shouting.'

He glanced over his shoulder. 'Did you see him?'

'See who?'

'Haines, he was standing right behind me.'

She stared into the fog, shook her head and sighed, then rested on her haunches. 'It's cold out here. Come on. Let's talk about it inside; you'll catch your death.'

12

Flynn told her what he'd seen. He kept repeating himself, as if re-enacting every step helped to make sense of it. Nia never said a word. She just sat and listened; didn't even ask how much he'd had to drink. Eventually, Flynn forced himself to shut up. And in the awkward silence that followed, he wondered if Nia thought he was crazy. 'Well?' he said.

'Well, what?'

'What d'you think?'

'I told you before. We need to get out of here. This place isn't good for you.'

There was a trace of desperation in her voice, and when Flynn looked up at her, her eyes were shining. He sighed into his hands. 'I know,' he said, dropping his hands onto his lap then raising his eyes to the ceiling as though searching for divine intervention. 'It's probably just the drink, me and my imagination. My dad was the same. I'll have forgotten about it by the morning.'

Nia sat next to him and held his hand. 'Come off it. We both know that's not true.'

He sat up. 'What the hell d'you mean?'

'You know what I mean, everything's that happened, your mother, Mason, and now this. It's all getting too much for you; which is understandable, considering everything you've been through.'

She gave him a long look. 'This place is no good for us anymore. I know I sound like a stuck record, but all this stuff, it's starting to scare me. And don't look at me like that, Ned. I don't understand it any more than you do.'

He wanted to laugh, renounce it all as drunken nonsense. If he'd met this version of himself months ago, he would have told himself to get a grip. 'I know what you're saying, but we still need to sit it out.'

Nia folded her arms across her chest. 'No, Ned, I've had enough of this.'

'You're just going to leave, go off on your own?'

'Yes, if I have to.'

The look on her face convinced him. Not that he had any doubts. He knew her well enough by now. He recognised that tone. The one that told him this was serious, and just you try to stop me. The realisation of what she was saying seemed to sober him up. Haines's reflection had been the catalyst. Yet this was worse somehow. Haines's ghost, or whatever it was, was little more than a shock, growing more ridiculous the longer he thought about it.

The notion that Nia would leave him was more frightening, the feeling intensifying as he pictured himself alone. He'd never felt like this, and didn't know what rattled him more, someone snatching her away from him, or becoming like all those desperate and needy fools before him.

'One more week,' he said, the words sounding pathetic the moment they came out of his mouth.

'No, Ned. No.'

He clenched his fists, suppressing the scream inside him. 'You know why. Come on, Nia, don't do this.'

'I'm going, Ned, and if you've got any sense, you'll come with me. I've been mentioning it for weeks now.'

He picked up a cushion and hurled it across the room. 'For Christ's sake, Nia. I need to sort things out with my mother. Haven't you been listening?'

'I have. I've listened to nothing but. We've waited long enough. We can settle-up with Simmons in the morning, we'll be out of here by midday.'

'And what then?'

'Then we'll take Bevan's car and start sorting things out for your mother.'

He stood, took a few steps towards the door, and banged his fist against the wall. 'It's not the right time yet?'

Nia walked over to him, and rested a hand on his shoulder, her cheek almost touching his. 'Yes, it is. What are you so afraid of?'

He struggled to explain it. It was a feeling more than anything, a foreboding sense that the time just wasn't right. A churning in his guts that, no matter how hard Nia tried to reason with him, refused to go away. 'Jesus, Nia, why are you doing this?'

'To help, I don't like what's happening to you.'

'And you think I do?'

'No, that's why we need to leave. No one's looking for you, Ned. It's been almost two months now.'

He watched the tears roll down her cheeks. He couldn't bear to see her like this. She was as tortured as he was. And if it was a choice between doing what she wanted or losing her. Then the answer was simple. He'd do whatever she asked. He'd never deny her a thing.

13

The plan had altered slightly because after Nia had tried to make an appointment with Simmons; they told her he couldn't see her until the following morning. Flynn was relieved to hear that. Even though they'd talked it through the entire night, and Nia had more or less convinced him, he was happy to get an extra day. He was in no rush, digging up that amount of money needed time and patience; he couldn't afford to be seen.

Flynn left the house just after midday, with a stomach full of breakfast. As he made his way to the woods, the fried eggs and bacon weighed on him. He quickened his pace, hoping to walk it off. If the weather was anything to go by, it promised to be a good day. A low sun loitered behind the trees, glowing across the swathes of fallen leaves. Traces of dew glistened on the grass, and in the distance, where the clouds almost brushed the fields, a low fog was rising. He'd miss all this, the vast openness of it all, the Hawthorns and the Sessile Oaks, standing beneath blue-grey skies.

Flynn smiled to himself, it wouldn't be that bad, swapping all this for a luxury apartment, and hot, sleepy afternoons on the beach. He held onto that thought as he took a left into the woods. Twists of dark ivy had grown over the track, and it took him a while to get his bearings. Then he caught sight of his mother's initials carved into the bark of a tree, taking one last look around before he walked towards it.

It didn't matter that there wasn't a living soul for miles; even the remotest places had to be approached with caution. Satisfied it was all clear, Flynn made his way through the trees, following each of his marks until he came to a small clearing. Long grass covered the spot, but he knew exactly where to dig. He'd thought about it every night, visualised the scene until it was etched into his memory.

Flynn stabbed the shovel into the ground, spat into his palms, then got to work. It took him a while to find his rhythm, but once he did, he dug like a man possessed. He didn't remember burying the money this deep, and though tired and soaked in sweat, he was glad he did. Occasionally, he stopped to catch his breath, catching a glimpse of something or hear a rustling in the trees. Before he'd left the cottage, Nia told him to take care. She sounded worried, as though warning him to stay clear of his ghosts.

Flynn kept digging for another fifteen minutes until he saw the frayed edges of the backpack. The sight of it slowed him down, and as soon as he'd loosened enough soil, he lay the shovel on the ground. He knelt, inhaling the rich smell of the earth, then cleared the remaining soil with his hands. Grabbing one of the shoulder straps, he lifted the backpack towards him, quickly unfastening the cord and pulling it open.

To his relief, everything appeared intact. The wads of notes were neatly stacked, and the gold rings and diamond necklaces glinted beneath the light. He stared at them in awe; the damp soil seeped into his skin; the voice in his head assured him it had all been worth it.

Flynn stood and slung the backpack over his shoulder, dropping to the ground as the gunshot exploded into the trees like a roar of thunder. Another shot quickly followed, only this time, it seemed closer. Flynn remained on the ground. He would stay there all day if he had to. In the unnerving silence that followed, he listened to the rapid thump of his heart. A bird clattered from the trees, and as he glanced up, he saw a figure on the bank.

Flynn couldn't tell if it was a man or a woman. All he could make out was that it was backing away, as though trying to keep its distance. Flynn seized his chance. He pushed himself up, checked the backpack was secure and started making his way through the trees, catching glimpses of the figure on the adjacent bank jogging alongside him.

Flynn headed east, where the trees tapered off, hoping to find a shortcut to the road. He broke into a sprint. Sharp blasts of air burned inside his throat, and his lungs felt ready to burst. He slowed down. His body reminding him he hadn't run like this for ages.

The wet ground squelched beneath his feet, and at one point, he almost slipped. To his relief, he finally caught sight of the road, a thin strip of asphalt cutting through the neighbouring fields. He'd never realised this part of the woods was so high up, and the drop from the retaining wall must have been at least twelve feet. He climbed over the wire fence and lowered himself onto the road, shifting the backpack into a more comfortable position before ascending the hill.

As Flynn came to the brow of the hill, parked in front of the Woods' entrance was a white Passat, with Ronnie, and some guy with a border collie, standing next to it. Ronnie had his hands on his hips, shaking his head as both men stared into the trees. They turned to face the road as Flynn drew closer. The man with the dog looked worried. Whereas Ronnie, as usual, was smiling.

14

'What the hell's up with you, Flynn?' Ronnie said. 'You look fit to drop. And what's with the backpack, never had you down as a Rambler?'

Flynn didn't answer. He just stared at Ronnie's flushed face, at the sweat stains on his shirt, and the scratches on his hands. 'Just been for a walk,' Flynn said. He glanced at the man with the dog, then up at the woods. 'What's going on?'

The man with the dog had answered before Ronnie had time to open his mouth. The guy looked to be in his late sixties, short and stocky, dressed in a green wax jacket with tufts of white hair sprouting from beneath his matching cap. He pointed at the trees. 'Gunshots, didn't you hear them?'

Before the man could continue, Ronnie interrupted. 'I'd stopped to take a leak. Those shots frightened the life out of me, almost pissed on my pants.' He glanced at the man. 'Then... sorry, I don't know your name.'

'Neil. I–'

'Then Neil passed by–both of us wondering what the hell all the noise was.'

Neil told his dog to quit whining and tugged on its lead. 'It was definitely a gun. But there's no hunting allowed around here. This place belongs to the Forestry Commission. I'm in two minds whether to call the police.'

'Makes sense, I suppose,' Ronnie said. 'Sounds like you're going to be a busy man. I'll let you crack on, Neil, don't want to get in your way.'

Either Neil hadn't understood Ronnie's hint or ignored it. Either way, he didn't budge. He just kept glancing over at the trees, shaking his head in contemplation.

Ronnie fixed him with a mean stare. 'Like I said, Neil, you best be off.' He nodded at Flynn. 'I need to have a private talk with my friend here.'

Neil seemed put out but didn't say a thing. There was no mistaking the threat in Ronnie's voice. Neil tugged the lead slightly, threw Flynn a nod, and started making his way down the hill. Flynn could hear him mumbling beneath his breath, but that was as far as Neil's protests went, and he had the good sense not to look over his shoulder. Sensing things were about to turn nasty, Flynn was glad to get rid of him too. They stood in silence, watching Neil until he was out of sight.

'So, what d'you want?' Flynn asked.

Ronnie forced a smile. 'Just want to chat with you, that's all. See how you're feeling after last night. There's no need to be so unfriendly.'

Flynn looked him in the eye. 'I'll chat with you later. I need to get on.' He stepped forward, pausing when Ronnie blocked his way. 'Don't be like that, Flynn. If you're in such a rush, I'll drive you.'

Flynn shook his head. 'I'd rather walk if that's okay with you?'

'No, it's not, actually. In fact, I'm feeling insulted.'

Flynn sighed. 'If you didn't want to feel insulted, then you should have been a better shot.'

'What's that supposed to mean?'

'You know what it means.'

Ronnie gave him a shove. 'No, I don't. All I know is that I don't like your tone, and you need to watch your mouth.'

For a second, Flynn thought about walking away. But he knew Ronnie wouldn't allow that, so he shot an uppercut into Ronnie's chin. Instead of going down as Flynn had expected, Ronnie spread his legs, balancing himself, then put his head down and leaned his weight against Flynn's shoulders. Then he grabbed Flynn's wrists, held them tight, driving them down whenever Flynn tried to swing a punch. They remained like this for a few minutes until Ronnie let go and started pounding the side of Flynn's head.

It felt as though Flynn was being smacked with a shovel. He hooked his foot behind Ronnie's leg, falling against him as they collapsed against the wooden gate. They grappled on the ground, using their fists, elbows, trying to gouge each other's eyes out, anything that gave them an edge. Flynn listened to the heaviness of his breath. Ronnie kept on at him, grunting and roaring, fighting relentlessly like a wild animal. Flynn head-butted the bridge of Ronnie's nose, saw the blood streaming into his mouth. It seemed to stun him for a second; Flynn did it again and, as Ronnie leaned back, gave him a sudden jab to the throat. He pressed his hands into the soil, kicking at Ronnie's shoulders until he squirmed free. Flynn tried to catch his breath, resting on his hands and knees, panting, crawling through the sodden leaves. When he glanced over his shoulder, Ronnie was already up. He was bent over, blood dripping from his nose, his hands resting on his thighs. As Flynn moved forward, Ronnie charged towards him, stopping Flynn in his tracks with a swift, hard kick in the guts. He followed through with another, dropping Flynn onto his back. He kicked him repeatedly before gripping his shoulders and turning him face down into the grass.

Flynn's legs felt like lead, and each breath was like a blade slicing into his chest. Ronnie pressed his knees into Flynn's spine, raised his arms and dragged the backpack from his shoulders. 'Jesus, Flynn,' he said with a laugh. 'Where did you get all this? You're definitely a sly one.' He jabbed the back of Flynn's head. 'And seeing as I'm feeling a little put out; it's only right that I take this as my compensation.'

Flynn tried to say something, but Ronnie punched him again before he could get his words out. 'Shut up. I've heard enough from you. You're like my dad, thinking the world's interested in your moaning.'

Flynn felt the pressure release from his back, biding his time as Ronnie crouched in front of him. 'You almost had me back there. Not bad for a dog that's had its day. I– '

Flynn pushed himself up, leapt onto Ronnie and bit a chunk of flesh from his ear. Ronnie cried out, his eyes wide with rage and shock. He tried to retaliate, but this time, Flynn was too quick, gripping Ronnie's throat, crushing it with all his strength, refusing to let go until he felt something crack. Ronnie's body went limp, and Flynn stared wistfully into his dead eyes.

15

Flynn lifted Ronnie's body onto his shoulder and carried it into the woods. Then he buried it in the same hole in the ground where he'd hidden the backpack. He still hadn't found the gun. He'd checked everywhere, even tried retracing Ronnie's steps. Its absence sickened him, confirming, perhaps, that once again his paranoia had won. Even if Ronnie hadn't been shooting at him in the woods, the fight was clearly his fault. Why had he been so keen to take offence? He'd acted like a different person. Yesterday, he'd been desperate to have Flynn as his friend, throwing him compliments, buying him drinks. Maybe hangovers made him mean. Or perhaps Bevan had mentioned that he'd seen Flynn in the woods, and Ronnie had gone sniffing around. That explained a lot. One of the best ways to learn a man's secrets was to get him drinking.

Flynn sat in the car, his hands shaking, his breath fogging the windows. It seemed so futile, that only hours ago he'd dreamed of a new life. A life built on hope. A vain desire that fate's warped humour inflicted on men like him should they ever try to delude themselves. Paradise was for dreamers. Hell was something he could touch. Every wrong turn as real as the blood and dirt that marred his fingers.

16

When Flynn pulled up outside the cottage, Nia was watching from the window. She dashed outside, probably wondering who it was. Flynn hurried out of the car, trying to reassure her. The sight of him held her dead in her tracks. She looked pale; there was a troubled look on her face.

'What's wrong?' he said.

'What's happened to you, Ned? Whose car's that? Have you been fighting?'

He glanced down at his hands, looking at the blood on his fingers. 'I had a slight fall, lost my footing in the woods.'

'And you just stumbled across a car?'

'It's Ronnie's.'

'Ronnie?'

'Bevan's nephew, he's stopping with him for a while. I'm surprised he never told you.'

She hesitated. 'That's right, I remember now, he mentioned something; it still doesn't explain what you're doing with his car.'

Flynn went silent, probing his mind for a plausible tale,

clasping to the first one he found. 'He's gone to sort out a bit of business, asked me to look after it.'

'What? He just went without his car?'

Flynn nodded. 'He asked me to drop him off at the station. I asked him why he wasn't driving, but all he said was *it's complicated*.'

Nia scanned the car. 'And you just left it at that?'

'I'm not one to pry, Nia, you know that. He seemed in a rush, kind of agitated.' Flynn forced a smile. 'It doesn't affect us. We'll be gone by tomorrow. All I have to do is leave it in Bevan's drive.'

'And Bevan knows about this?'

Flynn shook his head. 'I'll tell him later.'

Each time he opened his mouth, the lie took another turn for the worse. It was like a barbed hook, digging deeper, doing more damage the harder he tried to pull away. He could tell by the look on Nia's face that she didn't believe a word. She went along with it, though. He guessed she knew something was wrong but was keeping it to herself. Any curiosity she might have had vanished the minute she stared into the backpack. Nia fell silent, a gleam in her eyes, as though everything she'd ever dreamed of was now possible. She held her smile all the way to the cottage, and the moment they were inside, she asked Flynn to put the backpack on the table. She sat down, opened it slowly, and stared inside. It held her spellbound for a while. And Flynn had to say her name a few times before she answered him.

'I'm sorry,' she said, 'seeing all this, it's just...'

He sat beside her. 'You needn't explain. It gave me the same feeling.'

She plucked out a bundle of notes and spread them across the table. Then she took out a diamond necklace, closing her eyes as she let it slip through her fingers.

Flynn smoothed his hand across her thigh, started kissing her neck, working his way up to her mouth. She smelled of peaches, and it was a welcomed change from the damp, stolid smell of the woods. She moaned slightly as he pressed against her, and he could feel her nipples against his chest. He slipped a hand beneath her dress, resting it between her legs.

17

It was over sooner than he'd wished. In fact, it had finished quicker than his ego would allow. They lay together in silence, Nia's head resting on his chest. Flynn kept telling himself how tired he was. Things would be better tonight after he'd had some rest. The house stood quiet, brooding in the sulky half-light.

Flynn sighed, remaining silent when Nia asked him what was wrong. She was insistent, asking him the same question until he eventually gave in. He told her he was tired. What else could he say? That death followed him around. Mason was dead because of him. And now a young man's body lay buried in the woods.

He considered torching the car, in the faint hope that they would be miles away before anybody discovered it. It was a ludicrous idea. People would see the blaze for miles, catch the smell of burning rubber on the breeze. No, he would leave it where it was, and try to reassure Bevan in the morning.

He felt a stab of excitement. Only twelve more hours and

they'd finally be away. He eased his fingers through Nia's hair. 'What time are you seeing Simmons in the morning?'

'Bevan's picking me up at Nine, I should be home by half ten.'

'Why is Bevan taking you?'

'He offered. And it gives me a chance to say my goodbyes on the way.'

Flynn sighed. 'I don't know why you're bothering. If was up to me, we'd just go.'

'We've gone over this, Ned. I want to see the look on Simmons face. I don't want to owe *him* a *thing*.'

18

Nia's packing occupied her most of the night. Later, just after ten o'clock, she insisted on running Flynn a bath. He tried his best to dissuade her, but she refused to listen. 'You look drained. We've a lot to do tomorrow. Sort things out for your mother; we've a long journey ahead of us.'

Flynn smiled. 'We won't get my mother sorted in a day.'

'Exactly, so relax while you've got the chance.'

Flynn soaked in the bath for hours and kept topping it up with hot water. He felt like a king, watching the steam unfurl onto the landing, as Nia poured water down his back. Afterwards, he lay down naked on the bed, watching in silence as Nia lay next to him. Her aroma of perfume and wine comforted him. The slow rise and fall of her chest offered peace. 'Relax,' she said. 'You look troubled.' A hint of the maternal laced her voice, cutting through the wretchedness in Flynn's heart. The softness of her touch kneaded his skin. He basked in the magnificence of her touch, his eyes closing as he slid into a heavy sleep.

19

Flynn knew, even before 11:30 the next morning when Nia failed to return, she was lost to him. He'd waited for hours, chain-smoking, watching for her at the window. He kept calling her phone, and with every message his voice grew more frantic. She hadn't answered, and at first, he made excuses for her, kidding himself it was because of the poor reception. Even when he discovered the empty backpack, he played the fool, the black emptiness in his heart tinged with a drop of blind hope.

Flynn couldn't find Ronnie's car keys. Not that they'd be any use because on hurrying outside he noticed someone had slashed the tyres. Flynn ran. His body was trembling. All his fears, every imagined worse case scenario, were real now. Haines was more man than spirit. Nia's betrayal, her cruel deceit, was more haunting than any ghost. The earth moved quickly beneath him and only the thought of finding them, that savage redemption, stopped him from falling.

After a few miles, Flynn tired. He paused to catch his breath, tuning in to the faint rush of a car behind him. A red Ford Focus whizzed around the corner, and Flynn waved his arms wildly as he turned to face it. The car slowed to a crawl, stopping when Flynn ran towards it. The driver, a redheaded kid in his late teens, wound down the window. 'What's up, mate?' he said, the casual tone of his voice a harsh contrast to the unsettled look on his freckled face.

Flynn sat on his haunches, facing the driver's window. 'My car's broken down. I need to get to the village ASAP.'

The kid shook his head. 'Sorry, but I'm going left at the crossroads.'

Flynn sighed. 'Go on, pal, please. Do us a favour. I'll see you right when I get to the cashpoint.'

The kid thought about it for a second. 'The thing is, I'm already late.'

As Flynn was about to swing open the door and drag him outside, the kid said, 'Go on, then.' Flynn wasn't sure if the kid's sudden change of heart was through fear or shame. Either way, he didn't care. All he could think about was Nia, and the time he was losing as she drew further away. To his credit, the kid drove a steady 70, only slowing down for the bends. It still wasn't enough, and Flynn kept tapping the dashboard, growing more impatient. Eventually, they came to the village. 'Drop me by there,' Flynn said, pointing at Simmons's Estate Agents. He paused as he opened the door, turned around and tapped the kid's shoulder. 'What's your name?'

'Ali.'

'Thanks, Ali. I won't forget this. I'll see you right once everything's sorted.'

Ali didn't say a word, just nodded with a satisfied smile on his face. Flynn sensed the kid watching him as he stepped outside. The car still parked alongside the kerb as he shoved open the Estate Agent's door. To his relief,

Simmons sat at his desk, squinting over his half frame reading glasses as Flynn stomped towards him.

Simmons sat up. 'Mr Flynn, isn't it? How can I help you?'

He didn't seem as smug this time, but Flynn still didn't like him. 'I'm here to inquire about Nia.'

'Mrs Haines?'

The name still nettled him. 'Yeah, she came to see you this morning?'

Simmons leaned back into his chair. 'That's right, she came with Mr Cresswell. Paid any outstanding amounts and handed back their keys.'

'Cresswell. Hugh Cresswell?'

Simmons nodded.

'I was told he died years ago.'

Simmons shook his head. 'Thankfully, not. Unless it was his ghost that paid me this morning.'

Flynn frowned. 'Don't you mean, Bevan? Short stocky guy. In his sixties. Always wears a blue cap.'

'Yes, that's the man. But I can assure you his name is Hugh Cresswell. He's been renting a cottage from me. Contract's over now, of course. He accompanied Mrs Haines to return his key.'

'I thought that was his place,' Flynn said, 'told me he's lived in it most of his life.'

Simmons shook his head. 'No. Someone's taking you for a ride, Mr Flynn. He arrived here shortly after Mrs Haines. He was a good friend of her late husband. Didn't they tell you that?'

Flynn clenched his fists. 'Did either of them mention where they were going?'

'No. Why? I'm surprised you don't know.'

Flynn fixed him with a stare, watching Simmons blush.

'Can I ask where you're staying now, Mr Flynn?'

Simmons paused. 'The only reason I ask is I assumed you were leaving with Mrs Haines. The builders will start renovating in the morning.'

On catching sight of his reflection in the panelled glass, Flynn went silent. He stared into his own eyes. They looked wanton and confused. They were not the eyes of a man with blood on his hands, but those of an innocent child. For a moment, none of it seemed real.

'Mr Flynn?' Simmons said. 'Mr Flynn, are you all right?'

A huge emotion besieged him. Like a forgotten brother it forced its way out from the confines of his heart, trying to talk sense to the muddled thoughts that plagued his mind. He needed a way out, for his mother's sake at least. Flynn pictured the small wad of notes he'd hidden near the shed. 'I need to get some things from the cottage.'

Simmons nodded. 'Okay. I'll get you a spare key.'

'No, you need to drive me there now.'

Simmons leaned back into his chair and forced a laugh. 'I beg your pardon. I'm not driving you anywhere, get a taxi.'

Flynn gripped Simmons by the shoulders and slapped his face. 'I'd drive it myself, but that would be stealing.'

'I... I won't say anything, just take it.'

'I wish I could believe that, but as soon as my back's turned, you'll call the police.'

'Never,' Simmons said, his eyes watering.

Flynn slapped him again. 'Yes, you would. I've seen it so many times before, especially from squealing little runts like you.'

20

Simmons drove slowly, and Flynn had to keep reminding him to get a move on. The overpowering smell of the car's strawberry-scented air freshener did Flynn's headache no favours. He wound down the window, closing his eyes against the breeze. Sadly, the pleasure was short-lived, ruined by the faint blare of a police siren. Flynn sat up, checking the rear-view mirror before unclipping his seatbelt. The noise drew closer, and then, much to his relief, rang off into the distance.

Just before they reached the cottage, Simmons's car ran out of petrol. Flynn shot him a furious look, becoming more aggravated as Simmons wiped the sweat from his forehead. Flynn snapped his fingers. 'Give me your keys.'

'What?'

'Give me your keys and your phone. Come on, quick; don't make me ask you again.'

Simmons did as he was told. Flynn stepped out of the car, pausing before he closed the door. 'You stay here. Don't try anything silly now. I'm in no mood to give you another warning.'

'Sure,' Simmons said, 'I wouldn't dream of it.'

Flynn nodded and slammed the door, quickening his pace, looking back every minute, watching Simmons' moon-white face staring at the road ahead.

The shock of Bevan's involvement was easing. It all made sense now. Hindsight was a wonderful thing. From the moment Nia had her claws into him, they'd played him for a fool. He'd been blind to it all, manipulated at every twist and turn. Mason was right. Haines probably wasn't even dead, congratulating himself at how good he was at being a ghost. They hadn't planned on Ronnie dying though and, when he found them, he promised himself they'd end up the same way.

Flynn cried out. Anger, like a huge blister, swelled inside him. He didn't know whether to laugh or cry. Not that he had any choice. The approaching blare of the sirens didn't give him time to do either. Two police cars from opposite sides of the road charged towards him, forcing him onto the coastal path.

Haines had tipped them off, made that anonymous call, now that he'd enough distance. They wouldn't get rid of him that easily. And on that thought, Flynn broke into a sprint, holding the pace until the path tapered onto the beach.

The sound of dogs barking drew closer, and a blur of blue lights flashed in the distance. Flynn looked around, searching for another route quickly realising there was no way out. To his left stood the cliffs, with the endless, impenetrable sea to his right. Flynn fell to his knees, punching the ground until the pain proved too much, and blood and sand stuck to his swollen fingers. A low sun gleamed across the water, and he felt a sudden rush of sadness as the waves broke onto the shore. Flynn lay on his side and pressed his ear against the sand. There was neither the hint of a whistle or a tune. All he heard was the thick beat of his heart and the gruff sound of men's voices.

NED FLYNN'S STORY CONTINUES …

HIDDEN GRACE

Pre-order Now

Revenge is best served cold, but the road to retribution starts within…

In his quest to find those who double-crossed him, Ned Flynn seeks the help of retired small-time fence, Eddie Roscoe. But Eddie's services come with a price. If Flynn wants the information he needs, then he must help Eddie find his missing son.

As Flynn and Eddie retrace the lad's steps, they discover his disappearance is more sinister than they hoped and become embroiled in a world beyond their worst nightmares.

Can Flynn and Eddie survive, or are the hunters destined to remain the prey.

SAMPLE CHAPTER - HIDDEN GRACE

The police had detained him for ninety-three hours and they still couldn't prove a thing. Ned Flynn's involvement with John Mason's death remained a mystery; and anything linking him to Ronnie boy's disappearance was circumstantial. What use was an anonymous tip-off? As Flynn's lawyer pointed out, *they were grasping at straws; it was their word against his.* Flynn had been in and out of prison enough times to know the score. He kept his story consistent. Mason had hired him to find his estranged wife, Nia. Flynn and Nia had hit it off and had been a couple until she ran out on him.

'And what about John Mason's death?' asked DI Taylor.

Flynn shrugged. 'What about it?'

'Were you aware of it?'

'How couldn't I be, it was in all the local papers.'

'And Mrs Mason mentioned it?'

'Course she did. She was his ex-wife, for God's sake. She attended the funeral.'

'Was she upset?'

'Yeah, considering.'

'Considering what?'

'That he didn't treat her very well. He was a mean-spirited man by all accounts.'

'And you didn't like that?'

Flynn leaned back in his chair. 'Before my time, nothing to do with me. I'm not the jealous type. I never dwell on a woman's past.'

'That's hard to believe, Ned. Surely you had words with him.'

Flynn and his lawyer exchanged a glance. 'Nope,' Flynn said. 'We talked when I first took on the job. A few phone calls, perhaps. But after Nia and me became a thing, we never spoke.'

'And why is that?'

'Why do you think? I had no need. Never gave him a second thought until Nia went to his funeral.'

'You didn't like that?'

Flynn shook his head, smirked. 'Like's got nothing to do with it. It was Nia's business. It was up to her if she wanted to pay her respects.'

DI Taylor released a deep, exasperated sigh. 'And Nia Mason can corroborate that.'

'I guess.'

'And where is she now?'

Flynn shrugged. 'Your guess is as good as mine. Like I said before, she ran out on me.'

'Did you go after her?'

Flynn shook his head. 'It never crossed my mind. I had my own troubles to worry about.'

DI Taylor nodded. 'Your mother's illness.' He studied Flynn for a moment. 'Does the name Martin Haines mean anything to you?'

Flynn shook his head; his face impassive as his heart

pounded in his throat.

'Come off it,' DI Taylor scoffed. 'Nia Mason must have mentioned him.'

Flynn released a heavy sigh, but before he could utter a word, his lawyer interjected. 'Detective Inspector Taylor, Mrs Flynn, died just before my client was taken into custody. Both you and I know you've no evidence against him. You can't detain him much longer. Mr Flynn needs to mourn. The poor man needs to arrange his mother's funeral.'

~

Looking down at his mother, lying in the Chapel of Rest, was the saddest thing Flynn had seen. Her face looked gaunt and pale, a deflated mask with the life sucked out of it. The image would stay with him forever. Yet knowing that she had died alone would haunt him most. Nia and Haines were to blame for that. It wasn't just about the money now. They were the reason Flynn's mother died without her son to hold her hand. The reason she took her last breath in a ward full of strangers.

With wet eyes, Flynn stared down at his empty hands. He'd hound them without rest, force them to make amends, although deceit as costly as this was beyond redemption.

'Are you all right, Mr Flynn,' said the voice behind him. 'Take all the time you need. This must be very difficult for you.'

Flynn turned to meet the lanky, immaculately groomed undertaker standing before him. A detached coldness lingered in the man's eyes, affirming that for him death was all too familiar.

Flynn managed a half smile. 'Thanks, Mr Saunders. I'm

ok. It throws you a sucker punch every so often. You mentioned there were still a few things to sort out?'

'Hymns,' Saunders said in a pious tone. 'You need to choose the Hymns and let me know whether you want to say something at the service.'

'To be honest, Mr Saunders, speeches have never been my thing. I wouldn't know what to say.'

Saunders nodded. 'That's fine, Mr Flynn. I have to ask, but it's your choice. Whatever makes you comfortable.'

Flynn nodded in appreciation. 'As for hymns, my mother was the church goer. I'll have to take your lead on that.'

'Of course,' Saunders said with a flat smile. He pondered for a second. 'It was your lawyer who informed me you required the standard coffin and gown. We can upgrade if you want. But as you can appreciate, quality comes at a price.'

'Standard's fine,' Flynn said. 'I'll settle the bill once I've sold my mother's house.'

Greed flashed in Saunders' eyes. 'Of course, Mr Flynn, you take your time. I'd never dream of discussing payment at a time like this.' He shot Flynn the sincerest of smiles. 'Have you had any thoughts on the reception? A small buffet perhaps? We work closely with a few establishments. I can get you a good discount.'

Flynn glanced down at the floor. 'The thing is, these past few years, my mother kept to herself. I'm not sure if she had any friends. She mentioned no one to me.' Flynn took a deep breath. 'A reception's a nice idea, but except for me, you, the vicar and your ushers, I doubt if they'll be anyone else at the service.'

Saunders replied with a solemn smile. 'At least we'll lay her to rest alongside her husband. I imagine she'd find great comfort in that.'

Flynn failed to understand why. His old man had tormented his mother during her lifetime. Why let him do it for an eternity.

∼

Flynn sat on the end of his mother's bed and stared into the open wardrobe. He'd taken most of her clothes to the charity shop. All that survived were a few blouses, an old shoe box full of photographs, and a half drunken bottle of whisky. For medicinal purposes, she always insisted. *Helps me drop off at night*, Flynn could hear her say. *I like a drop in my tea.*

Flynn knelt on the carpet, reached into the wardrobe, and picked up the bottle of whisky. He unscrewed the cap, closing his eyes as he held the bottle to his lips. Saliva flooded his mouth. That sweet malty smell triggered a slew of bad memories. Flynn stood, marched into the bathroom, and poured the whisky down the sink. Booze turned men into fools. Keeping a clear head was paramount. He'd let his mother down when she needed him most. Only a weak man allowed himself to slip back into the drink; and only a lowlife disrespected his mother's memory.

Haines was such a man. The thought of confronting him, Nia too, plagued Flynn's days like a persistent dull ache.

Finding them seemed a hopeless task. All he could do was ask around. Someone was bound to know. People only looked out for themselves. He'd learned that the hard way. Loyalties can turn so swiftly for the right price.

AFTERWORD

Thanks for reading. If you **enjoyed this book,** please consider leaving **a review**. Reviews make a huge difference in helping new readers find the book.

ALSO BY MATH BIRD

A small town. A stack of hidden cash. The scorching summer of 1976.

In the long, hot drought of 1976, trash cans line the streets. The scorching heatwave makes people mean, almost bringing life to a standstill. Young loner Jay Ellis dreams of escape, fleeing the small-town prejudices and the endless bullying. So finding a briefcase full of cash seems the answer to all his prayers, as does the magnetic pull of the stranger, Nash, who rolls into town shortly after.

ABOUT THE AUTHOR

Math Bird is a British novelist and short story writer.

He's a member of the Crime Writers Association, and his work has aired on BBC Radio 4, Radio Wales, and Radio 4 Extra.

For more information:
www.mathbird.uk

Printed in Great Britain
by Amazon